*P*raise for Candii's Quest

"We all know The Non-Traditional Key Gullz as the first rock cover band to enter the World Records as having completed the rock band endless set list for both versions 2 and 3. But did you know that was only the beginning of their story? If you're a hardcore NTKG fan, then you can't miss this amazing new chapter in their lives!"
-The Mossy Stone

"Candii's Quest starts off as a sarcastic adventure novel filled with interesting locales and exciting soundtracks, but toward the end I had shed quite a few tears too. I can't recommend this book enough for anyone who loves musicals, pop and rock music, and a generally fun time."
-Edumatainment Weekly

"The Non-Traditional Key Gullz played the Romp Room earlier this year and made Rockopolis a part of their amazing journey. I'm sure you're all aware of the great change their visit to the Continent of the Jam Gods made for us. But if you're reading this and not a denizen of the Land of Rock, I won't spoil it any further. Read this book and rock on to the fullest!"
-Rockopolis Daily Star

"Yeah, these are some rocking gnarly dudes. What's that? You're writing a book about them? Oh yeah, I was there. I rode on top of their van and twirled a ginormous spoon. They rocked so hard I grew my muscles back. No, I'm not kidding. Are you recording this call? No, I don't give you permission to quote me!"
-The Spoonman

Candii's Quest

By

Daniel G. Chou

ISBN: 979-8-9884664-1-3

For my wife, Marci.

I think I finally gave you a good gift.

Contents

Setting the Stage

When I was asked to transcribe this account of The Non-Traditional Key Gullz (NTKG), I knew it was one of grand landscapes, great risks, and, most importantly, *music*. It would be careless of me not to ensure you were familiar with the basic anatomy of a song since I have written many portions of this manuscript utilizing that structure.

A 'verse' is a unique part of the song that tells the story. A 'pre-chorus' is a repeating build up to the chorus which follows it. A 'chorus' is the most recognizable part that repeats several times. A 'bridge' is musically, and sometimes lyrically, different than the rest of the song and leads into its conclusion, which is sometimes another chorus and sometimes a coda. A 'coda' is the conclusion when, in certain instances, it is different than the chorus.

It is important for you to know that no adventure involving the NTKG would be complete without the songs that literally drove the action. Narrative is interwoven within the music and I even share with you the song and artist that was covered by the world's greatest cover band. More often than not, each verse, chorus, or other song part will have its own accompanying text.

For additional clarity, each section will list its first and last accompanying lyric. If the section begins or ends with an instrumental, you'll see this symbol ♫ ♫ ♫. Rock on!

If you are reading my account without the recommended musical accompaniment, then a true fan of the legendary NTKG musical catalogue surely you are not. I have always found music and sound to be a mighty enhancer of all things and this book is no exception. The text alone may be a semi-humorous affair, but with the historically accurate musical back drop, it will cue you in on the emotional roller coaster our heroes felt surging through their fingers as they faced the rocking world's greatest challenges.

Even if you know the songs in your head and do not think you need to play them out loud, then maybe do it out of respect for them: Key Gullz, Thad Penguino, Sir Taco, and of course, Candii. Just listen. Let the music gently fade into the background of your attention.

Listening to the song's lyrics and reading at the same time is not necessary. The NTKG are a cover band after all. They are no more original authors of the lyrics they chose to sing than I am of the account I am about to share with you. They merely chose the most rockin' jams to psych themselves up when the power of music was required. Their account is the most important target of your attention, so just feel the music as you read along.

Now please, enjoy the latest quest partaken by The Non-Traditional Key Gullz, one that changed them and the Land of Rock forever.

1 No Tickets to Paradise

Twilight began to set upon the bountiful grassy plains of Candii's unicorn ranch. Twelve fenced-in plots, six hay silos, and one stable all surrounded her idyllic suburban ranch mansion. Each of her thirty unicorn's magic horns glimmered in the remaining sunlight as she brought them back from pasture.

The unicorns entered the stable and she recognized that she was at peace enjoying retirement as a Unicorn Rancher now many years after her last world tour with the internationally critically acclaimed band The Non-Traditional Key Gullz. It had been many years since their heyday when they rose from relative obscurity to one of the world's greatest rock cover bands. Candii still found ways to use her bass guitar skills in everyday life such as when she untangled her unicorn manes with freaky fast fingers or shoveled hay into their stalls at a pace that could only be described as rhythmically efficient.

She was ready to close the stall doors, but not before she tucked each unicorn in for the night. She gave each one a gentle pet and a quick kiss on the head.

"Oh dear Charlie, dear Phineas, dear Kevin, and dear Cookie. My good Glitter, good Rainbow, good Twinkle, and good Shimmer. Sleep tight my Dazzle, my Princess, my Spirit, and my Glitzy. Dream well ole Lovely, ole Rosy, ole Sunshine, and ole Starry."

"Be still sweet Happy, sweet Bright, sweet Bella, and sweet Joy. Rest your heads sleepy Delightful, sleepy Elegant, sleepy Charming, sleepy Prism, and sleepy Vixen. Dance in dream land my galloping Amazing, galloping Silly, galloping Fancy, and galloping Starlight."

And, of course, there was her dearest of all the unicorns, the beautiful royal purple equine. "Oh Sparkles, leader of my team of unicorns. Thank you for trusting me and helping the other unicorns to do the same."

Candii glanced back at her team as she neared the stable door. She wept grand tears of pure elation. "I just love you all so much!"

She was known for her intense feelings about everything. She had a true, all-embracing empathetic connection to her unicorns that could not be measured, analyzed, or explained by science. Thad Penguino had once tried. It could just not be quantified.

The unicorns responded in similar neighing and kicking theatrics as the love in the room rose to a joyous limit. Candii stepped out, wiping away her tears of joy, and said good night while she closed the stable doors.

"Unicorns are my life, gosh dog it!" Candii said while fist pumping like a fiend. How lucky she was to have an entire ranch to herself filled with her childhood dream animals. Few little girls ever grew up to be who they dreamed in this shifty, high-speed world where those in power were always looking to exploit the young and talented. She was lucky to find an honest group early in her career that she grew to call her family and achieved their wildest dreams together. Yet, there were many others who were not as fortunate and she did not know what to do about that. What could she do?

While pondering this familiar point of guilt, the presence of pure musical rock brushing past her cheek startled her. Normally such a feeling would elicit a shout of, "Heck yeah!", but something was wrong. This wind was filled with malice!

Swirling clouds drew her eyes above. The sky turned dreary. An inverse tornado opened a dizzying funnel into the sky and out of its center descended a fabulous being clad in a shimmering black cape and skirt, menacing steel corset, and surfing atop a flaming xylophone. Her full, luscious black hair flowed as if orchestrated by magical forces and her thrilling knee-high boots looked fierce and powerful. This woman flew down and hovered above Candii.

"Behold! It is I, Morgana Malevolent, grand queen and wizard of the rock heavens! Stand back as I take what I want!"

Morgana extended her hand toward the sky. A pair of xylophone mallets flashed into existence between her fingers. With a deft hand, she played a haunting tune on her floating xylophone. The roof of the stable lifted into the air and hurtled into the vortex above.

Rays of colorful light rose from inside the stable and into the vortex. Candii heard her unicorns as they neighed in fright. She swung the door open. To her horror, she saw the brilliant wispy light was emanating from her unicorn's horns. Their colors drained from their coats and their sparkles faded. Their magic was being siphoned.

Candii ran toward Starry and clasped her mane. The green shine turned into gray within her palm. "What is happening?" she cried.

Morgana cackled hovering above the ranch. "I have conscripted your unicorn's magic to power my wizarding ways. Thank you for caring for these unicorns so remarkably well. Their magic is *strong*! Now, if you could please stop screaming, I need to concentrate as I store each unicorn's magic into a powerful pearl casing for safe keeping."

Further down the line, Sparkles neighed frantically and kicked open his stall door. He galloped through the stable and past Candii as she hopped on his back. They burst out onto the yard and Sparkles reared with defiance. Candii held on with fright and patted Sparkles desperately, barely able to calm him.

She pointed up above at the evil queen. "Jump as high as you ever have toward that witch! I'll knock that magical xylophone right out of the sky!"

Sparkles leapt majestically into the air but a thick stream of magic flowed out of his body and into the vortex. He neighed madly being unable to muster enough remaining magic to reach her. Together they crashed onto the ground and Candii tumbled through the grass.

Morgana crowed as she fled into the vortex. "You'll never catch me or see your precious unicorn's magic again! All hail the Land of Rock, suckers!" She disappeared into the vortex as it shrank into oblivion. The wind stopped roaring, the new moon emerged again, and the colors of nature returned to their natural luster. All except for her gray, staggering unicorns.

Candii struggled to her feet. Her mind was swirling and her vision was blinded with rage. She scanned the sky but found no trace of the magical portal. She flung open the stable door and stood before her team. They now lacked their vibrancy and brilliance.

She called to them with fire and brimstone upon her tongue. "My unicorns, mark my words! I will get your magic back and bring justice to our ranch!"

She hurried to her home and packed her bags. From inside her ancient tour trunk, she unfurled a large Non-Traditional Key Gullz World Tour poster from her days far gone as a rock music legend. A sprawling tour schedule spanned the bottom section. She ran her finger slowly over all the locations as she knew she had heard of this place, the Land of Rock, before.

"Eureka!" Candii rushed into her magical artifacts room and retrieved an old and fraying map of the Continent of the Jam Gods. There on its eastern shore was the Land of Rock. The band briefly toured the island nation during their earliest days. The Land of Rock was unique among the other kingdom and provinces on the island in that it had no uniting government, just a collection of free cities and leaders. She recalled the wild-ness in the streets, the electrified crowds in the night clubs, and the extreme terrain that made it a lawless place where everyone was free to rock out to the fullest. It was a musical paradise.

She spun her magic globe, its enchantment waning without the unicorns, and was still able to scry a direct flight to the Land of Rock was all but impossible due to the enchanted weather effects. On this little globe, a cloud of pink miasma floated far off the coast of the southern United States at the island's loca-tion. She would need to charter a boat to its shores.

She changed out of her grungy farmhand clothes and into her signature not-pants hot pants and tiny black tank top. Before rushing out of her home, from which she had no idea when she would return to, she grabbed her bass guitar. She knew if she were to step foot on the Land of Rock once again that she would need to prove herself in the most rocking way.

2 The Railroad Blues

Candii awoke from her nap on a wooden floor. She was sprawled out, lying on top of a burlap blanket, aboard a train traveling down toward the Gulf of Mexico. While the travel accommodations were lacking, the low-profile transportation method of bumming a ride on an open train car allowed her to be sure Morgana would not see her coming. The Queen of Rock would surely watch for the name Candii on any incoming flight itinerary and notice if she were being followed. Candii could not give her the upper hand and needed to ensure an uneventful and safe trip to Louisiana where she would charter a boat to the Continent of the Jam Gods.

Candii gazed softly across the nighttime plains of the Midwest as the train slowly passed. She felt a song coming on and asked a hobo on the other side of the car to pass a frail acoustic guitar. Lead guitar was not her normal act, but she needed to warm up before she was ready to rock her bass. And right now her soul needed musical healing.

Begin City of New Orleans by Arlo Guthrie

VERSE 1

Riding ... mail.

Candii reflected on her journey today. Had it only been a few hours since she saw the most incredible of sights? She remembered growing up in Illinois as she plucked away an old folk song. The vibrations of the guitar relaxed her. The passing flowing wheat fields reminded her of the grain she grew at home for her unicorn team.

PRE-CHORUS

All ... automobiles.

Candii was fortunate enough to have a hay making machine, the latest in technology, in which she threw the grain and out popped fully bundled hay for equines. She heard there were similar machines for milk, wool, and eggs that made them into products like cloth and mayonnaise. Candii was not a country girl. She hated the outdoors, but technology sure made it easy to be a rancher.

CHORUS

Good ... done.

Candii's fingers played incredibly well considering how long it had been since she had performed. Years had passed since she shredded with sweet, hard rock. Would she be ready again now that her team needed her? There was only one way to find out and she was eager for the challenge.

VERSE 2

Dealin' ... floor.

Candii laughed as she remembered playing the card game Nertz with her new hobo friends earlier that day. They lost because no one beats the master hustler of Nertz. Even after a scathing loss, the hobos still shared their paper bag. The beverage was strong and it managed to hit all the right spots.

PRE-CHORUS

And ... feel.

The rhythm of the rails started to rock her to sleep. She dreamt of a magic carpet whisking her away to a sleepy dream land where none of this had ever happened. Candii felt the gentle beat of the wheels below her feet. The tempo coursed through her musical soul. She found her foot tapping outside of her control because music was so deep in her being.

CHORUS

Good ... done.

As the dead of night overtook the train car, everyone took a nap. Candii enjoyed the period of rest after having been on her feet and frantic for the last full day.

VERSE 3

Nighttime ... sea.

Candii jolted awake. She took advantage of a long stop in Tennessee to run into Graceland and visit the home of legendary rock and roll performer Elvis Presley. Being physically present in the rock legend's home filled her with the inspiration she needed to fuel her trip.

PRE-CHORUS

But ... blues.

In her dreams Candii fumed as she thought again about Morgana and her cruel, evil tricks. Morgana was so powerful. How could she ever stand against dark magic when she did not even have her magic unicorns at her side? Could the power of rock stand up to the arcane whispers of dark magic? Was this all a bad dream and if so, when would she wake up from it?

CHORUS

Good ... done.

As the train pulled into New Orleans, Candii admired the night lights of the harbor dimming in the early hours of dawn. She hoped she would have time to enjoy the pastries and culture of the French Quarter while she found a charter boat to take her. There was much to be done and so little time.

End City of New Orleans by Arlo Guthrie

Candii jumped out of the train car and looked around the yard filled with unloading crews and cranes. The rising morning sun painted the train yard with dancing shadows. She saw a familiar pair of knock-off plastic aviator sunglasses approaching. He was wearing a shirt with his namesake pictured on it.

"Sir Taco!"

"Candii!" Sir Taco embraced her and took her bags. "It's good to see you again. How have you been?"

"Everything was going great these last few years until yesterday. Thanks again for letting me crash at your place for a bit." They walked out of the train yard.

"It's my pleasure," Sir Taco assured. "You have to tell me what's going on as soon as we get home. Why abandon your home and why so incognito? That isn't the rock-hard NTKG way."

They sat in Sir Taco's kitchen. Sir Taco plated breakfast and Candii finished explaining her journey.

Still a lover of food, Sir Taco joyously served Candii large helpings of several dishes. "A stack of pancakes, a stuffed-to-the-brim omelet, seven pieces of perfectly crispy bacon, a side of fresh fruit, and coffee with cream and sugar just the way you like it."

"Thanks," she said with her eyes growing wide. His expectations were far larger than her stomach.

He stared. "Well? You're the guest. You got to take the first bite before I can start," he grinned from across the table with a plate of his own.

She politely took a bite. The flavor was divine. She would actually have no trouble putting it all away. With a full mouth, she said, "To wrap it all up, I must go to the Land of Rock to retrieve the thirty unicorn pearls that contain my team's magic. I'm not sure what resistance to expect, but I'm hoping to catch Morgana by surprise by laying low on my way there."

"I see." He nodded pensively.

She could tell his gears were turning as he stuffed his face. But what plotting did he need to do? Suddenly, she noticed a glint in Sir Taco's eye. She knew what he was considering.

"No. No, Sir Taco. Don't even think about it! I should do this on my own. We went our separate ways after the world tour because we were ready to start our own lives. I can't do this to you and tear you away from…"

She looked around and saw the house mostly in disarray. "…whatever it is you have going on here," she said as respectfully as possible.

He shrugged. "Eh. I get to eat crawfish and jambalaya every day of the year and sing with the best jazz and blues bands in the world. But to tell you the truth, after all these years, nothing beats playing with the old band. I want to do this."

Candii smiled and threw her hands up in resignation. "Fine, I guess I'll let you tag along. But it could be dangerous. The music is going to be hardcore. And besides, it's just you and me. We're not even close to jamming like the band."

Sir Taco took off his tinted glasses and Candii gasped. She had only seen him do that once before when the band said their goodbyes in what felt like a lifetime ago. "I like to think I can be relied on when my friends need help. And I believe I can think of two more who feel the same."

3 Don't Expect Talkin' When the Boat's Rockin'

Sir Taco gave Candii a grand tour of all the great architecture and cultural spots of New Orleans. During the day they walked the coast, visited a cemetery filled with the music legends of jazz and gospel, and at night they went to the airport for a very important rendezvous.

Candii anxiously watched the incoming flights for flight 0810. When it finally arrived, she ran over to the bag terminals to greet her friends. Two rock legends walked through the crowd signing autographs, shaking hands, and kissing babies. Sometimes they confused a baby for an autograph and vice versa.

"Thad! Key!" Candii cried. She leapt into the air and came crashing down on them both.

"Candii! Long time no see!" Thad gave her a big hug as he climbed back on his feet and pulled them both up. Still clinging to what he claimed to be the best time of his life, he sported a shirt with just the word *College* written on it.

"I've missed you so much I could murder you and take you home in a body bag!" Key said. Always one to make a statement, her rose patterned shirt was fun. "But I won't because I'm feeling generous."

"Thanks. I like being alive." Candii waved Sir Taco over and he shook their hands respectfully. She was grinning ear to ear. "How have you two been? Tell me everything!"

"Oh, you know. Fighting for social justice and equity. Just normal stuff," Key said with a slight nonchalant wave of the hand. "We've been on the road the last few years running anti-racist music camps for the youths."

Thad leaned against Key shoulder-to-shoulder. "And we're really sticking it to those bigoted hooligans."

Candii nodded warmly. "You two always were the dreamers."

Thad chuckled. "You flatter me, Candii."

Candii grabbed for their bags. Picking up what appeared to be a light one, she heaved it over her shoulder with some difficulty.

"Woah! Which one of you remembered to pack your antique brick collection?"

"Ah," said Thad. "That would most likely be our sack of money."

"What?" Candii threw the bag down. She now noticed it was a burlap sack with a giant dollar sign spray-painted on the side. "But why would anyone carry this around?"

"Sir Taco didn't give us a lot of details just saying you needed serious help. So either you needed help finding bodies or burying bodies."

Key walked ahead wheeling her own bags. "I said to him, '*Fistsfull of cash can solve both of those problems.*'"

Candi opened the sack filled with bricks of bound bills.

Sir Taco patted her back and offered his hand. "She's right, you know. Come on. Let's go."

Back at Sir Taco's house, Candii explained her journey again. Regarding the Land of Rock, her knowledge was limited. But Thad, an internet sleuth extraordinaire, was there to help.

"So, I looked up some expert sources," he waved his phone in his hand, "thank you first page of internet search results, and I know that only one charter boat service will bring us out to the Land of Rock. Once we get there, we can rent a tour bus and travel fairly inexpensively. I suggest we bring loads of cash so we don't leave a purchase trail."

Key nodded. "Good thinking." She opened a bag she was carrying and inside were mad stacks of fat cash.

"Where the heck did you get all that cash?" Candii shouted. She leaned over the bag.

Key flashed a tiny smirk. "The last person to ask me that has yet to be found by authorities. I'm going to keep this as my little secret."

She shut the bag and tucked it under a chair. "Listen. I've been thinking about this Morgana Malevolent and what exactly her deal is. My best guess is she is a psychopath since she has no empathy for you or your unicorns who are clearly very happy on your ranch."

Candii nodded. "Thank you."

"Excellent personality profile," Thad said. "I think it's time we take this band on the road."

The group bought four tickets aboard the SS Rock-a-Doodle-Doo. The questionable vessel floated into the harbor and looked more like a fishing boat than the cruise line it sold itself to be on the website. Blatant patch jobs lined the hull, it was half the documented length, and its anchor appeared permanently dragging behind it.

"I rock-a-doodle-don't want to get on that thing," Key said.

A gnarly sea-worthy captain waved them aboard. "Ahoy, land lubbers! Welcome aboard my pride and joy."

After the band loaded their instruments and speakers into the cabin below, they were surprised to realize they were the only passengers besides the crew.

"Holy bologna, kitty and pony. They don't seem to get a lot of customers, do they?" Candii asked as she opened a few cabin doors and found mostly empty rooms.

Thad was behind her on his phone. "I'm starting to get bad reception as we pull away from shore, but I thought I remembered seeing that they did get good reviews."

"What was the criteria?" Key asked. "Five stars as long as you weren't murdered?"

"This is weirding me out too much. Can we do something to get our mind off of this?" Candii asked. She remembered why they even had to put up with these dismal accommodations in the first place. "Ooo! I'm so mad just thinking of kicking Morgana's butt!"

Sir Taco pumped his fist into the air. "Yeah! After hearing about your encounter with her, I feel hungry for revenge!"

"Hungry like the wolf?" Thad asked as he unpacked their instruments.

Sir Taco grabbed his microphone. Thad tuned the lead guitar. Key arranged her drums and Candii whipped out her bass.

Begin Hungry Like the Wolf by Duran Duran

INTRODUCTION & VERSE 1

Dark ... dodo.

The nighttime darkness on the empty ocean gave the band a feeling of loneliness.

"Despite the calm waves, I'm feeling a fire well up inside of me!" Sir Taco growled.

"I know what you mean," Candii said. "Morgana won't be able to hold a candle to the combined rock power of The Non-Traditional Key Gullz!" She yelled into the great dark abyss. "Morgana! I'm gonna find you and then I'm gonna whoop your butt!"

Key got excited and started jumping around. She had a lot of energy to burn so she started kicking everything in sight. The band laughed and started to kick things too forgetting Key was sometimes a little too wild.

"Hey! Knock that off!" a deck hand shouted.

CHORUS

In ... wolf.

"Just like the song says, I'll touch YOUR ground, if you know what I'm saying," Key said. She winked about seventeen times.

"I'm a hungry wolf and I'm hungry for revenge!" Candii said.

"I'm just hungry for tacos," Sir Taco mumbled.

"I'm hungry for an adventure!" Thad said.

VERSE 2

Stalked ... dodo.

The late-night moon shone off the ocean water like a unicorn pearl. Candii saw the light shimmer and for a moment thought it really was indeed a pearl. A girl can dream, she thought.

"You feeling my heat?" Key asked, still taking everything up to the next level. She danced uncomfortably close to a deck hand who was clearly not interested. "Yeah? Yeah? I don't know what that's supposed to mean. I'm sorry everyone." She slinked away.

CHORUS

In ... wolf.

"Does anyone else smell that salty sea water? It's gross," Candii lamented. "Can't nature just keep to itself?"

"Let's drown out that smell with sound!" Thad turned up everyone's amps.

"I don't think that's how that works," Candii began to say until several of the ship's crew came up topside and started dancing to the music.

"Oh, you've heard of us, maybe?" Thad asked one of the deck hands playing a mean air guitar.

"Sure have!" she said. "I have all your albums on vinyl!"

INSTRUMENTAL

♫ ♫ ♫ ... wolf.

Even the ship's eye-patched captain ascended and brought her banjo to join the band.

"I knew I recognized you! You're The Non-Traditional Key Gullz! I'm a huge fan!" The captain laughed heartily and tuned her banjo. "I hope it's okay if I jam with you."

CHORUS x2

Burning ... alive.

The captain ripped some fiery chords on her banjo and her music resonated with the band. It was a folk match made in heaven.

"Wow! This captain can really make it happen!" Candii said.

"She even knows our songs!" Thad said.

The captain grinned. "Have you seen my quarters below deck? It's got Non-Traditional Key Gullz posters covering the walls!"

Candii threw a hand up. "Slap my hand!" They high fived. "I don't care if you're the only boat out to the Continent. I'd charter you any day!"

"You know, back when I was a landlubber, I used to rock out pretty hard," the captain said.

"Yeah, okay, grandma," Thad joked kindly.

"I used to be in a band called The Salty Sea Dawgs. I'll have to tell you about it some time," the captain said.

Key looked around suspiciously. "You can't all tell me no one noticed what the captain did there a minute ago. My quarters below deck? Come on, people!"

Everyone laughed.

End Hungry Like the Wolf by Duran Duran

After a night of killer jams, the captain invited the band to dine with her. She introduced herself as Captain Bing and they laughed and drank the night away.

Sometime in the middle of the night as the band slept, Candii awoke with a start. Something felt amiss. She jumped out of her bed and left the band's cabin. When she rose to the deck, she saw a single mop and bucket sliding alone across the deck as the ship tilted to and fro. Yet there were no crew to be found.

The bucket toppled over and brown, dirty water splashed everywhere. "Ha, the poop deck," Candii said.

Suddenly, the boat rocked and swayed violently. Candii grabbed onto the side railing before almost flinging overboard. As she stared into the black water just below her, she saw two giant glowing yellow eyes staring back at her. She screamed and fell back onto the deck. The ocean began to splash and the ship continued to rock as a giant octopus ascended from the depths and loomed over the small boat.

The rest of the band hurried onto the deck at the sound of her scream and gasped at the sight of the intimidating creature.

Sir Taco screamed like a banshee. "Oh gee willikers! It's a sea monster!"

The octopus replied, "Monster? Don't you think that's a bit harsh? I went to Yale."

Sir Taco cleared his throat. "Oh. My apologies."

Candii pushed Sir Taco out of the way and stomped across the bow. "What do you want, octopus? Let us pass to the Continent of the Jam Gods without incident!"

"I'm afraid I can't allow that," the octopus bellowed. "I've been ordered by Queen Morgana to stop your band from reaching the mainland. I hope you understand. It's nothing personal."

"You and what means?" Thad shook his fist menacingly.

"Oh you mean these?" Tentacles rose from the water holding an array of musical instruments. "Queen Morgana bestowed upon me a magical unicorn pearl that grants me the power to do grand things. I will use her gift to drum up the waves and overturn your boat. Then I shall be rewarded handsomely."

"Maybe you don't know who we are, you beast, so I'll introduce us." Candii struck a pose. Glitter inexplicably burst from a barrel behind her. The band assembled at her rear and instinctively posed despite totally not being choreographed. There was an exciting shimmer in the air. "We are The Non-Traditional Key Gullz and we will punish you!"

"I'm feeling pretty lucky with the power of the unicorn pearl," the octopus boasted.

"You'll need more than luck to flip this boat!" Candii said.

"You're right. How about a song?" the octopus asked.

Begin Get Lucky by Daft Punk ft. Pharrell & Nile Rodgers

INTRODUCTION & VERSE 1

Like ... beginning.

The octopus began playing his instruments and singing with a beautiful voice that surprised even Sir Taco and took Key's breath away. The unicorn pearl amplified his volume to new heights.

As the unicorn pearl floated above the octopus' head in the night sky, Candii realized she had mistaken it for the moon's reflection earlier. She had indeed spotted the pearl with her own eyes but she did not trust her gut. How naïve she was!

PRE-CHORUS

We've ... stars.

"I was in the all-male glee club in college. Does that surprise you?" the octopus asked. He splashed a tentacle to create a mean bass line that rocked the boat.

CHORUS

She's ... lucky.

Candii rallied the band and they began yanking ropes and battening down the hatches. They secured the lines and dropped the anchor even lower to help keep the ship oriented correctly. However, the waves began to violently batter the ship.

The octopus laughed. "You think a few adjustments will keep your dinghy afloat? Let me turn it up a little." He infused his instruments with more unicorn magic and they began to grow louder and the waves more furious.

VERSE 2

The ... it.

"What is all this racket!" Captain Bing yelled as she stepped out from her quarters only to see a giant octopus.

Thad went flying across the deck, being flung by the turbulence, and said, "We got a *rocktopus* on our hands and he's trying to overturn the boat with the power of his music!"

PRE-CHORUS

We've ... stars.

"Ding dang rocktopi and their flim flam music!" Captain Bing disappeared into her cabin momentarily, then emerged with her banjo and a huge amp so big that it took five deck hands to haul it topside. She plugged her banjo into the tall stack of amps. "What count is this monster on?"

CHORUS

She's ... lucky.

"Hey, you big dangly mess!" Captain Bing shouted at the octopus. "This isn't my first rocktopus rodeo, you know!" Huge waves splashed onto the deck as the surly captain strummed a jaunty chord. "Gotta jam them back into the sea!"

"Wow! I didn't know that banjo was electric," Candii said.

"It's a hybrid," Captain Bing winked as she started jamming out the exact same song as the octopus. The rocking of the boat began to lessen.

Feeling steady on her feet again, Candii screamed up at the clouds, "We're coming for you, Morgana!"

"I'm sorry," the octopus said. "I don't think she can hear you over the sound of my awesome rock!"

Instrumental

♫ ♫ ♫ ... *lucky.*

The crew took over the securing of the boat and let the band focus on helping Captain Bing.

Thad finally put two and two together. "Hey! Captain Bing's music is negating the octopus's musical sound waves!"

"We should get our instruments, too!" Sir Taco yelled as he ran down below deck.

Thad followed and they retrieved all their instruments. They plugged into Captain Bing's amps and began playing the song back at the exact same frequency and volume as the octopus.

An ominous storm cloud began forming up above as their fierce sound waves disrupted the local atmosphere. Lightning cracked and a light drizzle began to fall.

PRE-CHORUS

We've ... stars.

The octopus infused more power into the instruments and got louder. The band had trouble keeping up with his reverbing sound that started to again whip up some wild waves.

Candii stumbled around and almost dropped her guitar overboard. "Whoa! These waves are picking up again! Be careful and hold on!"

CHORUS

She's ... lucky.

"Hold on, crew!" Captain Bing said. She handed her banjo to her First Mate and ran to the ship's towering mast.

"But Captain! It's too dangerous to climb the mast in this weather!"

"Shush, boy! Let your Captain do what she must!" Captain Bing climbed the frightfully tall mast, with thunder and lightning crashing down into the ocean, and flipped a switch in the crow's nest. A lightning rod rose from the mast and took a massive crack of power from the heavens. The band's amps started to glow and grew even louder.

Astonished, the octopus turned to his unicorn pearl. "No! I need more power! Queen Morgana will literally turn me into sushi!" Try as it might, the pearl provided no more power. The octopus cried out in failure and abandoned his instruments, the pearl, and dived back into the dark abyss.

"Quick! Someone, grab the pearl!" Candii shouted.

End Get Lucky by Daft Punk ft. Pharrell & Nile Rodgers

Thad leapt off the deck and dived down into the water as the pearl splashed down. For a few tense moments everyone stared overboard as the light of the pearl descended into the darkness. Then it began to rise again and finally emerge in Thad's hands.

Captain Bing clapped. "By George! That was one heck of a dive!"

"I was an all-American diving champ in high school. That wasn't my best work, so there's no need to be impressed," Thad said.

"Oh my gosh, this guy!" Key cried at Thad being so extra.

Candii grabbed the unicorn pearl and felt its warm glass-like surface filling her with magic and love. "This one's for Charlie. We're going to do everything we can to rescue them all."

4 Disney Princesses, Eat Your Hearts Out

After waving goodbye to Captain Bing, the Continent of the Jam God's first impression was dismal. Gray, rocky landscapes, a volcano spewing a permanent haze into the sky, and withered black trees mostly spotted the horizon.

"I thought this was supposed to be a rock party paradise," Key said, holding a red plastic cup in her hand ready to party herself.

Thad checked his sources. "According to Climate and Geography Enthusiasts dot com, the rock lifestyle is like one big party and no party can last forever. There are parts of this province that have been burnt out for years."

The air took a noticeable evil turn. "How unfortunate, you poor sweet babies." A devilish cackle from behind surprised the band. They swiveled around and Morgana Malevolent waved coyly with one hand, floating in the sky and surrounded by twenty-nine hovering unicorn pearls.

Candii pointed sternly into the sky. "Give those back, you witch!"

"There's no need to go PG on me, darling. You now stand on the Continent of the Jam Gods where everything we do is hardcore. Swear if you must."

Key yelled, "You're a bobble-headed, lint licking bi…"

"Don't stoop to her level!" Candii pleaded.

Morgana cooed and fluttered her eyelashes. "Despite your restraint, compliment taken!"

"Now we have you where we want you! Prepare to be rocked!" Candii said. She ran to her instrument bag and unzipped her guitar.

"You really think you can touch me from down there?" Morgana scoffed. "Without your instruments unpacked and while I harness the power of twenty-nine unicorn pearls, you have no chance."

"Eh…she has a point," Key said.

"Well…um…I'm gonna…" Candii looked around frantically for anything she could use. She quickly picked up a rock and threw it.

Such a barbaric tactic caught Morgana off guard and she flinched. The rock hit her in the boob and one of the pearls separated from the pack. It plummeted toward the ground.

Candii caught it and held it tight.

"Curses, you rock plebe! I see strolling around outside with the pearls is a liability around you. I didn't want to do this, but so be it!" Morgana used her magic and sent the remaining twenty-eight unicorn pearls even higher into the sky. They resonated and glowed for a few moments. Morgana dramatically shot her hand into the sky, winced, and clasped her injured boob with her other hand just before firing the unicorn pearls in varying directions inward toward the province. Several of them wobbled and darted wildly as they shot through the sky.

"Rats! That didn't quite go as planned. I tried sending the unicorn pearls back to my castle, but some of them didn't fly as straight and narrow as I wished. Never mind that. My minions will gather them up and keep them safe until I can retrieve them." Morgana hovered higher and higher and cast a disdainful scowl upon the band. "Do not doubt that they will continue to assert my dominant rule over my people and that they will surely stop you if you interfere. I may not be able to hold all the power at the moment, but this is a satisfying, if not at least safe, alternative for the time being."

Candii shouted from the top of her lungs. "You think that will stop us? We'll get all thirty unicorn pearls, you just wait!"

"I'd like to see you try. At the least, it'll be amusing to watch!" Morgana cackled again and disappeared with a wave of her cape.

Candii unclutched her new pearl. She felt its radiating glow. "This is for Phineas."

He did not want to spoil Candii's moment, but Sir Taco noticed the sun passing through the sky as morning was becoming afternoon. "How are we going to figure out where all these pearls flew to?"

"I already reserved a van at a nearby town," Thad said as he tapped on his cell phone. "I just pulled up the directions and it's about a half an hour walk south. Let's head there and load up our gear in the van. Once we get reliable transportation, we can figure out how to track them."

The band swung their luggage over their backs and started the long trek to the nearest town. During the walk Candii fumed about Morgana's arrogance. "Can you believe the nerve of her? She greets us just to mock us. Did she just assume we'd be powerless in her presence?"

"That's not an entirely false statement," Thad said as he navigated via GPS.

Candii kept turning in her mind how peaceful and perfect things were on her unicorn ranch. Everything was safe and idyllic. Each day was the same over and over. She got angrier and felt more insulted about this game Morgana was playing and it was all at the expense of her unicorn's happiness. She had it all going for her until Morgana ruined it!

She threw out her arm. "Sir Taco! Hand me my bass!"

Begin Rolling in the Deep by Adele

VERSE 1

There's ... dark.

Candii bristled with resentment. She knew the journey ahead would only get harder. "She was literally standing right in front of us! If only I was a little faster..."

"Or taller?" Sir Taco asked. "But that won't magically happen, so don't be so hard on yourself." He patted her back soothingly.

"Don't worry about it, Candii. We're going to beat her!" Key said.

"They'll be nothing left when we're done with her!" Thad said.

Candii nodded. "Ha, yeah. Just think: what can she possibly do against all four of us with our instruments?"

"That's the spirit!" Key said.

PRE-CHORUS

The ... feeling.

"Yeah! She tore my unicorn's happiness away! It hurts and I'm going to use that scar in my heart to wreck her!" Candii said.

Sir Taco was sad for Candii so he belted out the words to express how he thought Candii felt.

CHORUS

We ... beat.

"You had it all!" Sir Taco cried. "Now you're rolling in the deep! And it's all because of Morgana!"

The band continued down the road and noticed the trees and the grass swaying to their music. The Land of Rock had music running through its soul and it recognized good music when it heard it.

Sir Taco wondered if every province of the Continent of the Jam Gods was like this.

VERSE 3

Baby ... shared.

Thad looked up Morgana on the local web. "I see that Morgana has glowing reviews in the Land of Rock. However, she is rated quite poorly on accounts originating in other kingdoms and provinces."

"Sounds like someone is fudging the numbers," Key said.

As they crossed under a lush verdant forest canopy, Candii jammed hard and woodland creatures joined in.

PRE-CHORUS

The ... feeling.

Charcoal black squirrels and woodpeckers danced and tapped to the beat. When Thad's GPS lost its connection briefly, the band got turned around somewhere and lost their way in the woods.

As thanks for their musical stylings and free entertainment, the musical woodland creatures came to their aid. The band formed a conga line behind the animals and danced their way back to the road.

CHORUS x2

We ... beating.

Candii handed her bass to a passing black deer that was surprisingly adept at playing a musical instrument with its antlers.

"On the Continent of the Jam Gods, almost everything is musically inclined!" Key said.

The band sound-checked their instruments and amps and made sure they were in top shape. Sir Taco matched his pitch and gave the band a thumbs up. They felt unstoppable and knew Morgana should watch her back.

Candii felt a lot better.

BRIDGE 1

Throw ... sow!

"Ooo, when I get my hands on Morgana...I'm gonna...I'm gonna..." Candii growled.

"Save the performance for the show," Thad said.

"I just have so much pent up emotion and I want to let it out!" she cried.

BRIDGE 2

We ... all.

"Oh, you'll have your chance," he said.

"No! I just got to let it out!" she shouted. Candii burst with emotion, grabbed Sir Taco's microphone, and sang! "Me and my unicorns, we could have had it all, it all, it all, it all!"

CHORUS x2

We ... beat.

They approached Jammertown as Candii belted her heart out. This fairly normal-looking modern city was themed black and blue. They jammed through the streets with their battery-powered amps blasting from their backs. They searched for the address of the vehicle rental store. People opened their front doors and windows to witness the traveling rock concert. They waved and cheered the band on.

Thad led them to a vehicle rental business where they greeted a forty-something metal head who looked like he lived in his mom's basement. Candii wrapped up her song as the metal head patiently waited behind the counter and just enjoyed the show.

End Rolling in the Deep by Adele

"Welcome to Killer Solo Vehicle Rentals. My name's Krawl. Will you be renting for domestic travel within the Land of Rock or do you plan on visiting the neighboring Synth Kingdom, Death Province, or the Hair Band Republic?"

"Just domestic," Thad said.

"Do you have a reservation?" Krawl pushed his black bangs out of his eyes. Key noticed his fingers twitching slightly.

"We have one tour van." Thad gave him their reservation number.

"Righteous. Are you sure you don't want to take any other type of vehicle?" Krawl asked as he rummaged through a drawer of keys.

Thad scratched his head. "Um..."

"I'm just messing with ya! We don't have any other type! I'll pull your van around and meet you up front." Krawl grabbed keys and headed out a back door.

"Well, that was an interesting guy," Key said. "Did anyone else notice..."

"The twitchy fingers?" Candii asked. "It was like he was holding back from wiggling them uncontrollably. Very weird!"

Thad confidently said, "Maybe he's a guitar player and he just loves...killer solos."

Out front, Krawl pulled up a tour van that was big enough for everything they had and then some. They loaded their items and Thad signed a mountain of paperwork.

"So, what methods of payment do you take?" he asked as the pen fell out of his cramping hand.

"Tourists, eh? Well it all depends on how talented you all are. I can take bills in Continent Cash or you can play me..." Krawl's fingers began twitching wildly again, "...one killer solo."

"Are you, like, addicted to solos? Do you need help?" Candii asked incredulously.

"No, no! I don't need help. I can stop anytime! I just...I'm a little hard up since Queen Morgana outlawed guitar solos in Jammertown."

Candii laughed. "Why would anyone do that?"

"Eh, she's not the biggest fan of me...for reasons." His eyes shifted rapidly back and forth. "So, how about that solo?"

"I think we'll stick to cash." Key opened her money sack and pulled out wads of bills. "How much?"

"Oh, no can do, seniorita. I don't take mainland bills, only Continent Cash."

"Well, where can I get these exchanged into…"

"Not feasible, I'm afraid. The nearest currency exchange is about two hours into the next province. So, then." Krawl rapped his fingers together. "About that solo…"

Thad pulled out his lead guitar and shredded notes like a rock god.

Krawl was drooling by the end. "Yes! Yes, that'll do very nicely. Here's a receipt for your deposit. The rest is due whenever you return." He twirled the van keys around on his finger. "Okay, so who is going to be the official driver?"

The band looked at each other and everyone looked confused but Candii.

"Wait. Am I the only one with a driver's license?" she asked.

"I live in the city so I haven't renewed one in years," Sir Taco said.

Thad and Key shrugged. "We haven't needed to drive ourselves for a long time. We fly and charter town cars everywhere," Key said.

Krawl slapped the keys into Candii's hand. "Looks like you're up, buttercup."

5 Beep Boop, Doing the Robot is Cool Again

Can you hand me those unicorn pearls?" Thad asked. From the wheel, Candii passed the two she had back to him. He touched them to his GPS. "I thought so. I know where we need to go first."

"How did you manage that?" Sir Taco asked either half asleep or half paying attention. You could never tell with his tinted glasses on.

"The magic of the unicorn pearls is telling my GPS where the other ones are. They all have a matching resonance frequency. It's like how Candii can tell which pearl belongs to which unicorn. They can communicate via their vibrations." Thad moved the pearls around until he received the strongest signal.

"And you didn't use Wikipedia to figure that out? Color me impressed!" Key said.

The band drove through the southernmost part of the Land of Rock. Thad directed Candii to an eastern city along the shore named Styxville. A unicorn pearl was broadcasting loud and clear.

Upon arriving, the city surprised them as it was themed in robot decor.

"Mr. Roboto," Key said. Everyone saw the inspiration.

Thad watched his GPS. "It looks like we're coming up to the pearl. It should be right around the corner so take the next left."

Candii turned the corner which appeared to be a one-way street. A hotel stood at the end of the drive. "This has got to be it."

"Yeah. This makes sense," Thad said.

Sir Taco sprung to life and leapt out the van's window. "Grab your instruments, amps, and let's head inside! I'm ready for action!"

The band hustled through the front doors with guitars, drums, and a small set of travel amps overflowing in their arms. The robot theme inside the lobby was disappointingly tacky. Large robot head chandeliers, chrome plated everything, and even a person poorly dressed in a robot costume made of common brown cardboard managed the reception desk.

Candii approached and decided to try the most direct route. "Excuse me, er...sir or ma'am, but I'm looking for your nearest unicorn pearl. Can you point me in the direction of..."

The robot quickly ducked under the counter and lifted up a large boom box. It dropped it onto the desk and pressed play. An old cassette inside started to spin.

"Sugar salted pits," Candii said with a frown.

Begin Popcorn by Hot Butter

VERSE 1

Popping begins.

The robot concierge spoke in a very bad robot accent. "Are you prepared...*cough*...for absolute devastation? Beep boop." It pantomimed a series of poorly choreographed robot dance moves that just made everyone feel embarrassed for it.

Candii raised an eyebrow. "Is this for real?" She watched the fake robot closely for any sign of breaking character. The robot did not break character. A piece of its cardboard shoulder armor began to slip. It quickly reset its armor without diverting its red LED light gaze.

"Are we being punked?" Sir Taco surveyed the room but didn't see any cameras. "Maybe this is a distraction."

Key shook her head. "It didn't even try to make real robot sounds. It just literally said 'beep' and 'boop'."

"We should probably just ignore it and move on." Thad made his way down a nearby hallway but was startled when scores of doors swung open dramatically to his left and his right.

VERSE 2

Drumming begins.

A horde of cardboard clad robots stumbled into the hallway and blocked the path forward for the band.

"Look there! Way in the back!" Candii pointed beyond the robots at a pair of elevators. "That's where we need to go."

"This is nuts!" Key laughed nervously. "Just push past them!" She tried to force her way into the robot horde but was overwhelmed by their collective push back. "That's no good! Is there any other way through?"

Sir Taco surveyed the lobby again. "No. It looks like this is the only way to get further inside the hotel."

"How are we going to get past these creeps?" Key asked.

"Let's blow them out of the way! Arm your amps!" Candii said.

The band laid down their amps and plugged in their instruments. They adjusted their straps, grabbed their picks, drumsticks, and mic, and turned the knobs to their safest max, level ten!

CHORUS

♫♫♫

The robots were startled and felt the pressure of the sound waves pushing back on their cardboard armor. They collectively leaned forward into the music and linked arms against the reverb.

"They're holding on!" Sir Taco said. "At this rate, they'll just stay put indefinitely!"

"I'm as loud as I'm going to get!" Candii said.

"We don't need volume," Key yelled. "We need science!" She railed on the cymbal sending specialized high frequency sound waves through their cardboard and into their hearts.

The robots collectively let out, "Heck yeah!" and Key knew she had them.

"That's it! Keep up the novel groove!" Key said.

VERSE 3

Popping resumes.

The robots began to shudder at the pure awesome rock talent in front of them. With no one to play more rocking music on their behalf, one by one they began to slowly fall apart, cardboard piece by cardboard piece revealing normal, fleshy people underneath the costumes.

The front desk robot appeared behind the band holding the boom box high over its head in a feeble attempt to increase the volume. The band turned to face it and matched its boom box tone for tone. The robot leaned forward and the band leaned right back until the robot began tapping its foot. Their jam was just too good for it to ignore!

With that slight lapse in focus, the band gave it their all and blasted every piece of cardboard right off its silly body. All that was left was a woman shaking in her laser beam themed underwear.

"I'll take Queen Morgana's beatings instead of dying here! Bing bang!" She threw the boom box on the ground and fled right out the front door. Her minions quickly followed, half-clothed and shaking in their remaining cardboard armor.

End Popcorn by Hot Butter

"That is one messed up dress code. I would definitely not apply if I knew that was their corporate policy," Sir Taco said.

"Enough talk. Let's storm the building!" Candii led the charge as the band rushed the elevator and fit themselves and their instruments into a space that was clearly not designed for them. The door closed and everyone sucked in their stomachs.

"Pretty cozy, ain't it?" Key squeezed herself toward the floor buttons. "Hmm. Let's see. First floor...tenth...the Rock House?" She pressed the Rock House button and the elevator sprung to life at a breakneck speed.

Candii screamed. "Oh my gosh! We're gonna die!"

Everyone yelled until the elevator came to a screeching halt. The floor was announced over an intercom. "Top floor. The Rock House. Rock on to the fullest, my dudes."

The door slid open and the band sprung out like a jack-in-the-box.

Candii opened her eyes and felt her face pressed against white marble floors. "Someone at least has good taste." She picked herself up and took in the beautiful sight of diamond, gold, stone, and gemstones decorating every facet of this wealthy penthouse suite.

"Holy wow. I'd hate to take a guess at the nightly rate for a room like this!" Sir Taco said.

"More than you can afford. Buzz, whirr…" whispered a voice from high above. From atop a crystal staircase stood a towering figure draped in a luxurious bathrobe. A tall and slender cardboard-adorned robotic woman descended the steps slowly. A futuristic visor covered her eyes. She clapped twice and a gleaming chandelier came to life.

The walls of the penthouse illuminated slowly inch by inch. Across the back wall, mounted black diamonds sparkled to life spelling out the name *Roboxy*.

"I was warned strangers might come for that. Beep boop." Roboxy gestured to the top of the chandelier upon which a shining unicorn pearl sat. "That's why I put it high out of reach."

"Quick! Grab the pearl and let's get out of here!" Thad said.

Candii took off her shoe and chucked it at the chandelier. Roboxy's eyes widened and everyone held their breath as, in slow motion, the shoe hurtled toward the center of the chandelier in a perfect spiral. It smashed into a large center crystal ball and rocked the chandelier back and forth.

"Nooooooo!" Roboxy yelled in a low slow-motion tone as she stumbled down the stairs and tried to position herself under the chandelier.

Seeing that Roboxy was lining up to catch the pearl, Key also sprinted toward the chandelier.

The unicorn pearl slowly rolled out from its seat and gently bounced through the chandelier's arms like a Plinko board. With their eyes too focused on the prize, Roboxy and Key collided in an incredible slow-motion crash.

"Whyyy isss everythinggg innn slowww motionnn?" Thad asked.

"Becauseeee it'sss sooo epiccc!" Sir Taco said, watching with bated breath.

The pearl fell in between them and bounced away toward a large floor-to-ceiling window.

"No. It wouldn't," Roboxy said anxiously. The unicorn pearl rolled quickly to the glass and tapped it. The clink caused a small crack. Everyone held their breath until the unthinkable happened: the glass shattered and the pearl rolled out.

"No! It'll break!" Candii darted quickly and pushed through Key and Roboxy. She ran at full speed toward the now gaping window.

"You're crazy, girl! Let the power go!" Roboxy yelled, but Candii refused to listen. She leapt out the window of a one-hundred story tall hotel and dived after the tiny pearl.

The wind whipped through Candii's hair and her eyes teared up as she plummeted several stories per second until she reached out and grabbed the pearl. She felt the warm glow on her freezing hands.

"This is for Kevin!"

She was quickly approaching the ground and she did not have a plan. She shut her eyes and wished for a miracle when suddenly she was surrounded by a magical bubble of light. The bubble drastically slowed her speed and gently placed her down on the street before dissipating.

Candii pushed the unicorn pearl tightly into her chest and whispered, "Thank you, Kevin."

The rest of the band burst out of the hotel's door. They whooped and hollered with excitement. Roboxy walked out behind them.

"Thank goodness you're okay!" Key said. She hugged Candii tightly and held on tight. "What were you thinking, you big, bumbling bumble bee?"

Sir Taco laughed and slapped Candii on the back. "If you're ever going to jump out of a window again, let me know. I actually like base jumping!"

Roboxy approached the band. They reached for their instruments. She raised her hand in deference. The band relaxed.

"You are one crazy dame," Roboxy said. "Sometimes we have power placed into our laps and other times we earn it. I was doing well before that pearl fell into my lap. Those spoils of war were earned. But what I have now is not mine. I can see that you are far more deserving than I. Take the unicorn pearl. Just leave me and Styxville be."

"Deal." Candii threw out her hand and Roboxy enthusiastically shook it. With the type of respect befitting of two masterminds, their palms clasped tightly together as they smiled. "Can I go back in and get my shoe?"

"Ha, ha. No. I'll send one of my minions to retrieve it for you." Roboxy walked away and mumbled quietly to herself. "Rock gods, watch over us. Queen Morgana will hear about my failure."

6 Rock Never Sounded Sweeter

I had continued to navigate with Candii at the wheel. "The next nearest unicorn pearl is sort of on top of a mountain, if I'm reading this GPS correctly. Let's head for a small, unmarked village at the base and see if we can find a way to the top."

The band pulled into a small medievalesque village complete with farm animals and cloth cap wearing peasants. However, one thing was notably unique: all the buildings were made from confectionary. It resembled a gingerbread village.

The van's wheels got stuck in the mud road. Everyone had to get out and push.

Key slipped and fell on her face. She lifted herself up with a huge grin on her face. "The mud is chocolate!" She dived back in.

"I can assist you strange visitors." A passing man, dressed in magical robes with a long wizard beard, rolled up his sleeves and whipped out a wand. After a short incantation, the van lifted out of the mud and levitated to dry land. "There you are. Please avoid the potholes as you pass through Candy Mountain. Good day."

"Candy Mountain?" Candii asked.

"That's right. You stand in the street of Candy Town at the base of Candy Mountain. Perhaps you are here as tourists and wish to visit the ice cream summit?"

"Why, yes. That's exactly why we're here," Sir Taco said.

"Ah! Well then welcome to our humble home. However, I regret to inform you that the summit is off limits due to an ice cream avalanche brought upon us by Queen Morgana for our insolence. Since winter is setting in, it's unlikely the ice cream will melt and clear the road to the top."

"I thought everything was all rock and roll out here. What's with the candy?" Thad asked.

"Ah." The wizard looked sad. "Well, rock candy used to complement our music, but Queen Morgana took all our instruments and left us with just the candy. She said her army of minions needed them more than we did."

Thad checked his GPS again. "The ice cream summit complicates things. That is exactly where we need to go."

"Shoot." Sir Taco said. "Well, wizard, let's say we needed to get to the summit really bad. Like, *real* bad. How could we do that?"

"Well, there is one person who maybe could help, but he hasn't cleared an ice cream avalanche in years. He's old now, you see. But what's the harm in asking?"

The wizard used his wand to carve a map of the town's streets in the chocolate ground. "Go down two streets and take a right. The house at the end of the cul-de-sac is where you will find the only person I can think of that can help you on your journey."

Candii smiled from the driver's seat. "Thank you, kind wizard. You know, for all the absurdity and hardcoreness of the Land of Rock, Candy Town seems pretty low key."

"On the surface?" The wizard raised an eyebrow. "Sure. However, the entire town is built on a giant vein of rock candy. I think that's pretty hardcore." The wizard waved and went on his way.

The band parked their van in the cul-de-sac and identified the house in question.

"Looks like a haunted house!" Sir Taco said.

Candii shivered. "I don't want to think about that. We'll go check it out. Thad and Key, keep the van running."

Candii and Sir Taco walked up a long wooden staircase and shook a huge door knocker. The clack, clack, clack was heard echoing through what sounded like an empty house.

"I guess nobody's home," Candii said far too quickly as she turned and started to run back toward the van. Sir Taco remained and he reached for the doorknob. Before he touched it, the door unlocked from the inside and slowly opened.

"Yes? Who's there?" A tiny wrinkled man appeared. He tried adjusting his glasses but his eyesight was so poor that it did not help.

"Hello, sir," Sir Taco said. "We were hoping to get help reaching the top of Candy Mountain. A wizard told us that an ice cream avalanche made the road impassable and that we might find help if we came to this house."

Candii slowly inched back toward the door.

"An ice cream avalanche, you say?" The old man furrowed his brow. "Hmm. I haven't dealt with one of those in say…fifteen years. I'm not as strong as I used to be!" He lifted his cane and swung it about, but his back cracked and he settled down. "I would love to clear the road for you, but I'm just too weak."

"Maybe you could lend us your tools and we could just dig our way up to the top?"

"No, that wouldn't do. I'm the only one that knows how to wield my tool."

"I'm sorry, old man. I wish there was something we could do to make you young again."

"Old? I'm not that old. I'm only twenty-nine!"

"What?"

"Oh, that's right. I probably look decrepit, don't I? I haven't seen myself in a mirror for years since my eyesight started to go. No, I'm not old. I'm just weak."

"Well then old man…I mean weak man…I mean, I don't know what to call you. Just tell us what you need."

He tapped his cane rhythmically on the porch. "Rock. I need good ole fashioned rock to fill my soul. Candy Town has been devoid of good rock for years. The only rock that remains is of the candy variety, but man cannot live on rock candy alone. No. This man needs a steady diet of fire and brimstone across the chords of a guitar."

"Well, okay! We're the right people for the job!" Candii perked up and offered a handshake. The man obliged. "It's nice to meet you. My name's Candii and we are The Non-Traditional Key Gullz. We can rock for you."

"Okay! Let me go grab my equipment, it'll be just a second!"

Candii and Sir Taco returned to the van and waited until the man exited his house. Filled with excitement, he moved too quickly and tripped down the stairs barreling down all the way to the van.

"Oh my goodness! Are you okay?" Candii asked leaping out of the van.

"I'll be fine!" he waved assuredly. "Let's just get this show on the road. Help me up on the roof of your van and head up to the mountain top. If you rock hard enough, I should be ready to eat all the ice cream and clear your path." The man proudly brandished a giant spoon, the only tool he needed.

"Well, okay then!" Candii helped the man climb on top of the van and ensured he felt steady. "The band and I were talking and we wanted to play you a song that really resonated with you. Do you mind if I get to know you a little better? What's your name?"

"I'm the Spoonman."

"Say no more." Candii jumped into the driver's seat and hoped that she could drive and play the bass at the same time.

Begin Spoonman by Soundgarden

INTRODUCTION & VERSE 1

Feel ... Spoonman.

Candii kicked the van into high gear and sent candy gravel flying across the drive as they tore out of the cul-de-sac.

"Yes! I feel the adrenaline! Go faster!" the Spoonman yelled into the passenger side window. He gripped the van top with his frail hands to prevent himself from being flung off.

"If you say so!" Candii put her foot down and popped a wheelie with the van.

"Woah!" Sir Taco said. "Is he still up there?" He stuck his head out the window.

"Sure am, rock man!" The Spoonman smiled and flashed a peace sign.

Their tires turned the street into blazing hot chocolate. Townsfolk whooped and hollered as they left a rocktastic sound wave in their wake. Candii carved a path up to the mountain road.

CHORUS

Spoonman ... oh.

"Ooo, I'm feeling it! But I'm going to need years of your music at this rate!"

"Rock harder!" Candii barked as she plucked her bass with one hand and gripped the steering wheel with her other.

Sir Taco held onto Candii's guitar neck as he belted into the microphone.

VERSE 2

All ... oooh.

"Yes, that's it! I feel the youth returning to my bones!" the Spoonman howled into the sky.

"Did you just say all your friends are skeletons?" Key laughed. "Ooo! Spooky!"

CHORUS

Spoonman ... your.

"Sing until your lungs give out!" the Spoonman pleaded. He felt steady on his feet like he had not in years. He lifted his spoon into the air and twirled it like a baton. "Forward, Non-Traditional Key Gullz. Forward! Ha, ha, ha!"

They barreled past a sign, *Candy Mountain summit this way.* They shot into a chocolate tunnel and burst out the other side spraying sprinkles all over the mountain side. The road then became narrow and twisting.

BRIDGE

Come ... on.

Sir Taco had to take a breath, so Thad took the mic and whispered a few *come ons* to keep the vibe going.

"Hold on, people!" Candii twisted the wheel wildly to stay on the winding road covered in melted ice cream.

The Spoonman rooted his spoon on the van roof to steady himself. "Woah! I like your energy!" he said.

Sir Taco took back the mic and Thad started his guitar solo. He shredded the chords and checked to see if the Spoonman was enjoying it. Thad could not believe his eyes. Spoonman looked thirty years younger!

"Yes! I feel stronger already!" The Spoonman said.

INSTRUMENTAL 1

With ... ♫ ♫ ♫

Key took the lead and laid down a solid beat for the band.

The Spoonman let out a loud shriek. "Yaaas! I feel my power welling up inside!" He grew two feet taller, his beard receded, his hair turned jet black, and he grew formidable biceps.

INSTRUMENTAL 2

Spoons begin clacking ... off!

Flurries of coconut shaving snowflakes began fluttering around them as the road became slippery. Candii held the steering wheel with an iron grip and tried her best to keep the van level. The wheels spun and the van swerved inches from the death-inducing edge, but she continued to keep her cool.

Finally, they reached a huge ice cream pile roadblock with cherries on top and she slammed on the brakes.

CHORUS

Spoonman ... Spoonman.

The side of the van collided with the massive mounds and the Spoonman was jettisoned into the air.

"Spoonman!" Candii shrieked as his flailing body tumbled into the sky and disappeared into the cotton candy clouds.

"This is where I jump into action!" The Spoonman somersaulted out of the clouds and landed in front of the huge ice cream pile with his giant spoon at the ready. He scooped spoonful after spoonful into his mouth. With fury and focus, he devoured the entire roadblock within a minute.

He was a hungry boy.

End Spoonman by Soundgarden

Sir Taco marveled at the clear path ahead now devoid of more ice cream than any one person should ever be able to devour. "I have never in my life seen anyone eat something that big so fast!"

Thad laughed. "Spoonman, did you hear that? That's a real compliment coming from him!"

Candii dashed up the mountain road and climbed to the summit. There, resting on top of a ginormous scoop of chocolate moose tracks, sat the unicorn pearl like a cherry. She plucked it out and licked the tasty treat clean. "This one's for Cookie."

Once she returned to the band, the Spoonman said, "Glorious rock band, thank you for restoring my youth and power. I can now once again serve Candy Town for the foreseeable future. The path ahead of you is clear. May whatever you are seeking be within your grasp." He leapt into the sky one last time and dived off the mountain side. "Good day!" his last words echoed.

The band gasped and peered over the edge. Far down below, the Spoonman surfed on his giant spoon, descending gracefully but also super hardcore, down the mountain.

"What a man…a Spoonman," Key cooed.

7 Ice, Ice, Living

Thad tried putting more unicorn pearls on his phone. "It doesn't seem that Cookie's pearl from Candy Mountain or Kevin's from Roboxy gives my GPS any more power. Which I suppose is fine because we're getting a very good signal as is."

"But we need to be quicker," Candii said. "Every moment longer means more unicorn suffering."

"I understand your frustration, but we need to be cautious at least for our next stop. Candy Mountain was crazy but our next experience is going to be even colder. We need to go deep into a wasteland tundra. There are two unicorn pearls under ice."

"Oh boy. Hopefully not literally."

"There is a very high chance."

Candii slumped behind the wheel. "Nothing is going to be easy on this trip, is it? Well, if that's where we have to go, then here we go." Candii turned at the next intersection and drove them toward a blinding white horizon.

After about an hour, the depressing landscape they left behind seemed almost welcoming compared to the cold indifference of its fierce western tundra. The band bundled up with what few meager clothes they had packed as the van got colder.

"The Land of Rock does not disappoint when its tourist brochures say everything here is hardcore," Key said. She tried to peer out the frosted window but could not wipe away the ice building up on the inside. "Hey, the heat is on, right? I feel like it's just as cold in here as it is out there."

Candii tried to find an outside temperature gauge but the van was too old and did not have one. She held her hand over the air vents but felt nothing.

"Hmm... we may have a problem," she said. Despite the snow on the side of the road, Candii pulled over and toggled all the heat switches.

Sir Taco poked his head up front. "What's going on?"

"I think the heat's been off for a while now, but it was so gradual I don't think any of us noticed there was a problem."

"Now that you mention it, I think my hands are numb." Sir Taco wiggled his fingers. "Yep, definitely numb."

"Okay, let me just try..." The car's engine shut off. She checked the engine temperature gauge and saw it was deep into the cold mark. "I think the engine just froze."

"What do we do?" Key asked, wrapped up like a burrito in a freezer.

Thad checked his GPS. "I'm not sure if this is good or bad luck but we are not very far from one of the pearls. It's maybe ten minutes down this road and it's in the middle of a lake."

"It's possible it's sitting on top of the ice," Sir Taco said.

"It may also be twenty feet under. Let me try calling Krawl at the van rental and see if we can get a tow." Thad called while the rest of the band huddled together to stave off the chilling winds slipping into the van.

Begin Hold Each Other by A Great Big World ft. Futuristic

INTRODUCTION & VERSE 1

I ... oh!

"Hello, this is Thad. We rented the tour van earlier today. We're stuck in a snowbank and our battery is dead. Can we get a tow and a battery repair? Uh huh. I don't remember."

"What's Krawl asking?" Sir Taco asked.

Thad cupped the phone. "He wants to know if we bought the snowbank or frozen battery insurance."

"Well, that's rather specific. Where's the receipt?" Sir Taco began digging around the van looking for it.

CHORUS

Something ... other.

"I'm getting colder. I think I can't feel my toes now," Candii said. "I'm so worried and frustrated. What if you all die out here because of me?"

"Scoot in closer," Key offered from inside her sweater wrap. Candii climbed into the back and squeezed in close to warm up, but one of the windows would not roll up all the way and the breeze was cutting through their jackets like a knife.

Sir Taco's fingers had trouble feeling anything under the van's seats. He just wildly yanked anything he felt. "Why are there so many empty bags of Tias chips?"

VERSE 2

Everything ... oh!

"Can we retroactively purchase snowbank and frozen battery insurance? No? That would defeat the purpose of insurance? Well, what do you suggest, *sir*?"

Candii's breathing began to slow. Her mind was beginning to fog and her eyes blinking slower and slower. "I can't believe this is happening. I'm so sorry, everyone. I'm so…"

Key remembered her phone had a weather app. She checked. "It's twenty degrees below freezing outside, everyone. This is bad!"

Sir Taco noticed Candii was barely breathing at all. "Is she okay? Candii?"

Key tried to shake her awake but Candii fell limp. "Folks, we have a problem! I think she overexerted herself with empathy for us!"

CHORUS

Something … other.

Everyone took off their light jackets and wrapped them around Candii.

Sir Taco opened the glove box and found the receipt. "Here it is! Let's see…we do *not* have the snowbank or frozen battery insurance." He threw the receipt at Thad.

Thad swatted it away. "Listen! We're freezing out here! I don't care how much it costs. Just help us get a tow!"

Sir Taco put his hands on Candii's cheeks but they were so cold. He felt her slightly moving ensuring she was still breathing, but barely.

VERSE 3

Yo … okay.

"Thank you!" Thad hung up his phone. "Krawl will be out here with a tow helicopter in fifteen minutes."

"That's service!" Key said.

Candii slowly began to warm up and breathe more steadily. Everyone began to shiver so they huddled around Candii.

"Are we going to make it fifteen minutes like this?" Key asked.

"Keep yourself awake. Just don't fall asleep," Thad said.

"Sir Taco, sing us a song," Candii muttered with half-opened eyes.

BRIDGE 1

I ... now.

Sir Taco sang to the band.

BRIDGE 2

You ... you.

Sir Taco sang to Candii.

CHORUS

Something ... other.

Sir Taco laughed. "Of course that goes for all of you." He giggled a little, but his teeth hurt from the cold so he stopped.

"That goes without saying," Key said. She wanted to say more but was losing consciousness.

Sir Taco's lips turned blue and he felt like he could not keep singing.

Key wanted to ask for another song, but she could not inhale enough air in her frozen lungs to speak.

Thad forgot what was so important about staying awake and he fell asleep.

They stayed huddled in a ball.

End Hold Each Other by A Great Big World

8 The Magic School of Hard Knocks

Oh, Jayce. I can't wait until graduation! We'll both finally be out from under the thumb of the headmistress. We'll start planning our future together."

Young Morgana Benevolent stared dreamily at her one and only, Jayce Corgimiester. Together they lounged in the grassy courtyard of the Boston College of Magic in the province of Classics. Other students spoke softly while pointing. As an enigmatic, relative newcomer to the province, Jayce's interest in her was a curious puzzle to others.

They didn't care. They were carefree.

Jayce listened intently. "Yes. We'll have much to arrange after we pass our qualifying exams."

Morgana dreamed of her life with Jayce in the big city. "We'll move to Rockopolis and start our own magic therapy practice."

Jayce laughed. "You really think you can start treating people just like that? I thought we agreed on both going to magical medical school first."

"Well, yes…" Morgana shifted uncomfortably in the grass. "I've actually been meaning to bring that up again. I just keep thinking we don't need to waste our time with more schooling. We're already top of our class, are we not?"

Jayce sighed at the thought. He leaned in closer and whispered, "Based on pure magical potency, certainly you are unrivaled among our peers. But your scores only reflect your prowess of your destruction magic and not the sorry state of your healing magic. Morgana. We agreed to master our light magic first, not to engage in a trial-by-fire in the real world." He reached out and placed his hand on her cheek. "Your father was an educated healer. You told me he valued education more than anything."

"That's not what he meant." Morgana scowled and rolled away. "Light magic isn't bound to books and hallways of education. Learning to be kind, to channel the light within can happen anywhere. You have to discover where to look, grasp what you want, and never look back. I'm done studying. I want to *act* and to *grow* stronger!"

His face flushed. "I've heard enough. You're placing the cart before the horse! I'm sorry, but it's ridiculous to believe you can turn your destruction into light just by winging it. Only your studies can see to that."

Morgana's heart thumped. A sharp sense of fear pierced it. Jayce was talking about a very private and embarrassing issue in front of all the students in the courtyard. How could he?

She was suspicious of this 'more-schooling' racket he and her professors tried to sell. Fulfilling a promise made to her mother, she was close to completing her rudimentary education. But was more of her short, young life truly necessary? Her mother worked in enchanted law years before she obtained her formal degree. Certainly the same was possible in mystical medicine.

Her shaking fingers pushed her bangs out of her eyes. "*Please.* Someone might hear and..."

He threw out his arms. "Morgana, no." His hands scooped up hers in view of all the whispering gossips.

She turned red. He was coddling her. She could sense it.

"Your challenges are not something to be ashamed of. Plenty of wizards and witches find success through tutoring. Yes, channeling joy is difficult for you now, but with enough help…"

Her fingers vacated his touch. "You don't think that a senior at the top of her class can lift herself up? That she isn't capable?" How insulting. If anyone in this world should have believed in her, she thought it would be him.

These last few ears of her adult life had been wasted standing still and listening to the insistent jabbering of old fogies in robes and stupid ceremonial hats. It was finally time for them to start living life!

"We are more than capable, the both of us! There's no need for more *education*. Do you not fear of what supposedly comes after magical medical school? Will the elders try to wrangle us into higher medical education? Superior school? I can't keep waiting to grasp freedom! Our destiny is now our own!"

Jayce slouched and sighed. "Morgana, you're wonderful and talented. But no amount of innate aptitude is going to compensate for the trauma you've been through."

A witch nearby laughed with her friend. Morgana was sure they were laughing at her.

She rose from the grass. She wanted to be anywhere but here but Jayce caught her arm.

"We need masterful training from the best sources! We need more discipline!"

Their raised voices were beginning to attract unwanted attention.

Discipline? Was he alluding to that infuriating rumor about her childhood? That she was raised by trolls in the forest? Well...it wasn't entirely untrue, but such a reputation didn't help her here.

She cast him aside and twisted away. "Why are you doing this? You're binding me down, restraining my spirit! I told you before: never again! *Never*!" A red glow grew from her face, arms, and legs.

Jayce jumped to his feet. He scanned the courtyard frantically for a professor. Other students noticed steam radiating from Morgana's skin. The grass around them turned brown and wilted.

"Oh, I see it now," Morgana said, freely feeding a burning feeling at the bottom of her gut. "It's all clear. You knew I wouldn't follow you to med school. That's why you're so intent on going! You think I'm a lost cause just like everybody else says in this stuck-up academy. If you wanted to break-up with me, you should have the runes to *say it to my face*!"

"Morgana!" Jayce shouted, straining his throat. His vocal cords felt parched from the intense heat she exuded. "You need to calm down! You're losing control again!" He tried reaching for her hand. "Honey...!"

"Don't touch me!" A blast of searing air pushed him and other students onto the ground. Her heart filled with fear and rage. Without a conscious effort, she hovered into the air. Her vision blurred and painful memories of her past replayed reminding her of a seemingly eternal hopelessness.

Students began to flee. It wasn't that long ago when Morgana last lost control on the campus. All the ashes in the science wing still hadn't been cleaned up.

"No, my love! I won't let you give in to fear again!" Jayce fell to his knees. He carved runes into the dirt with his fingers. Stones under the surface scraped and drew blood as he winced.

The sweltering oven she was constructing singed the tips of his hair. His friend, Tim, waded into the chaos and grabbed his shoulder.

"Jayce! She can't be saved, man! Let's..."

Morgana growled. Another blast of blistering wind flung Tim into the sky. Jayce watched as Tim fell painfully upon stone outside of the courtyard. Muttering under his breath, Jayce tried to complete his binding spell but he could not bring himself to do as she had accused him of. He knew of her past and what freedoms were stolen from her. He could not sequester her ever again.

"Please, *someone*!" he pleaded to those running as fast as they could. "Get the professors! I can't...!"

Flagstones twirled out of their path, molten earth oozed onto the surface, and the clouds turned a deep, crimson red. A pillar of flames erupted and curled down off the emerging magical barrier hastily being channeled around it.

Morgana's consciousness returned. Bright lights bathed her vision. She recoiled and blocked the shine with her hand. "Ugh. What happened?" A thin sheet covered her body. She knew she was no longer in the courtyard. "Where am I?"

A blurry figure loomed over her. "She's awake. Take her vitals."

Double vision merged into one. The crisscrossing wooden rafters of the infirmary echoed murmurs and cries of pain from others.

"Slather more aloe fast!" demanded someone from across the room.

"I need a level-three ice spell on bed thirteen!"

Her thoughts were swirling. This puzzling transition from an argument to the infirmary left questions in between. The argument...

"Jayce!" She shot up in bed. "Where is Jayce? Oh my goodness, what is happening?" Mind aflutter and her gut in knots, guilt poured over her from what little she did recall.

She kicked her sheets off and started to glow a brilliant red. Nurses from all over the room dropped their instruments and abandoned their patients to descend on her. Some grabbed her arms and legs while others chanted incantations to cool her body and muddle her mind.

"Let...go of me!" She cried. "Jayce! Where is he?"

"He's here! He's right over there!" the head nurse screamed, sprinting across the floor. She gripped Morgana's bedside, out of breath, and smiled when Morgana began to settle back down. "Look, just over there as cool as a cucumber."

Morgana spotted Jayce breathing, lying unconscious on a stone slab in the center of the room. Three nurses whispered constant incantations at his side. A shroud of crystalline blue magic encapsulated his body.

"Jayce!" A reverberating wave of chaotic, crackling heat magic thrust the staff back. She stumbled toward him finding her legs to be weak.

The staff picked themselves off the floor. Cautiously, they surrounded her. The head nurse waved them back. So instead, they pointed their magic defensively toward Morgana from a safe distance.

Morgana fell at Jayce's side. She reached out for his hand but her fingers brushed against the glass-like barrier. She pressed her palm upon it frosting her fingertips. Jayce looked serene but injured. The hair from his head was gone. His skin smoldered a bright blood-orange red.

"What's wrong with him?" she cried as she threw herself over his prison. "Who did this to him?"

The nurses exchanged nervous glances. None of them volunteered the obvious answer.

Tears splashed onto the barrier. Frozen crystals sprinkled to the floor and shattered. Other than her sobs, the room grew silent. "What happened? What transpired in that courtyard?"

The ward's double doors smashed with a thunderous crack into the wall. Morgana whipped her head up. Her tears sizzled and evaporated as they dripped down her cheeks. Headmistress Irma Sotomayor's notorious heels clacked against the white tile floor. One after another, the nurses lowered their hands. The calvary had arrived.

"He's in an alchemistic-induced coma concealed in an arcane aura of freezing stabilization," Sotomayor said. She stood at Morgana's side and glanced over Jayce's body. Her upper lip curled; brow furrowed. "He'll probably never wake up."

"You're lying," Morgana whispered, burying her face in her hands.

"What I say is true." The walls amplified the impatient tapping of her shoe. She shifted her broad shoulders toward Morgana. *"You* did this to him."

"No!" Morgana faced Sotomayor with reddened eyes. "I was…I had everything under control. I was just upset and letting off steam. I…" Her memories failed to show her more.

"Ms. Benevolent, in reality, *your* outburst almost cooked him alive. I and the faculty managed to pause his decline. He'll remain in this frozen state until we can find a way to stop your flames from burning his body from the inside-out the moment we release the spell."

"Do it now!" Morgana twirled and snarled. "I know as headmistresses you have the power. Don't patronize me and claim that you don't, that every moment further he suffers is because of me and not your inability to act."

Sotomayor scowled. "You think Jayce would still be like this if I *could* do anything about it?" She slammed a first upon the barrier. A powerful rippling wave emanated out. Only the staff shuddered as it passed through their bodies. Morgana and Sotomayor stood unfazed. "No. Magic like that doesn't exist. I've spent the last few tumultuous hours contacting sorcerers all over the continent." She directed her gaze oppressively upon Morgana. "*None* of them can so much as fathom a strategy that can reverse the unbridled rage you directed into his body."

"Then…then…" Was this truly her mess? Surely there was someone else to blame, she being the victim of misfortune and cruelty all her life. It could not be true that she was now the one hurting others. It was outlandish. Unfair.

If there was any shred of truth to what the headmistress said, Morgana perhaps had a responsibility. She rolled up her robe's sleeves and placed her hands hastily upon the crystal. The cool kiss almost made it too painful to sustain contact, but for Jayce, the discomfort was trivial.

"I made this mess. I'll do it!" she announced.

Sotomayor slapped Morgana's hands away. "You child! You're like a volcano of undisciplined emotions! You could no more heal a person than you could cast sustained light magic out of a single finger. You are nothing but an unrefined failure!"

Morgana stumbled back. She was too startled to respond.

Sotomayor gazed at Jayce's blue face. "He was our top student. His skills were just starting to take form. He could have brought immense pride and recognition to the college. And his father, he will never forgive us…forgive me." She placed her hand on the crystal. It curled into a fist. "I told him to dump *you* like a bad habit. He refused and now look at what happened!"

Morgana covered her eyes and shook her head wildly. "No, no, no! I don't want to hurt people! I just want to help! I just want to heal!"

With a menacing scowl, she spun toward Morgana. She cast a quivering finger upon her. "This is *your* fault. You are a chaotic danger. You must be reined in for the safety of the land."

The nurses backed away and several fled into the hallway.

"H…H-headmistress," the head nurse mumbled, placing a finger on her shoulder. "I think it's best if we let the student disciplinary process do its job."

"I *am* the disciplinary process." In a moment of weakness that would haunt Sotomayor for the rest of her life, she let slip from her lips the first few words of a vengeful incantation upon a student.

Morgana's arms began to tingle. A force gripped her elbows and bent them backwards in a binding position. As she recognized what was happening, she leapt back putting several paces between her and the most powerful sorcerer she knew. She shook of the binding but felt other energies hovering around her.

"You dare be an enemy of the light? I only wish for good, healing, and peace!" She shook her head. "I would never hurt Jayce on purpose or any of the other students! This was all an accident. This is why I came to the college! You were supposed to *help* me!"

Morgana swirled her fingers and cast a wall of fire between the two to keep them separated. The flames were poorly controlled. Bed sheets and curtains were ignited by mistake. She gasped. "Oh no!"

"You are beyond help, Morgana Benevolent." Sotomayor reached to the ceiling and thrusted down a gust of smoke extinguishing the flames.

Morgana stumbled to the floor. She coughed and struggled to breath. A frightening childhood memory turned her heart into a drum. She felt like she was going to die unless she escaped what she believed was the burning apartment she was trapped once again in.

"You won't keep me as your pet any longer! I will be *free* and you will pay!" Morgana blew a magic gust from her lungs and dispelled the smoke. The wind did not stop and furniture lifted into the air. The few students too sick to flee were flung out of bed.

Sotomayor casted floating spells as quickly as she could and whisked the students out the windows. "You're a menace! Everything you do leads to ruin!"

The taunt returning her to the present, shame cascaded over her shoulders. She hated the feeling and had to prove the headmistress wrong. If she failed to do so in this most critical of moments, then perhaps she truly was lost.

"I'll show you! I can be the light! I can do so much more!" Her fingers twitched wildly as she muttered an angelic enchantment. Her eyes concentrated on the glowing white ball forming in her hands as it flashed between light and darkness. To her dismay, spurts of fiery embers sprung from the ball. She twisted her wrists and contorted her neck in an attempt to redirect her magical intention, but her heart was filled more with fear and anger than the healing spirit she desired.

Seeing the desperation in Morgana's eyes overtake her anger, Sotomayor understood the error in her previous intention. Maybe Morgana would never find the light inside of her, but that did not make her eligible for judgement by a woman who had failed to help.

Sotomayor ordered the nurses back into the room. "Secure Morgana in a detention hex! On my mark!"

They formed a circle around Morgana, lost in her own failing incantation, and scraped their arms with their nails to offer up sacrifices for such a powerful bewitchment. The scent of blood filled the room.

Morgana's ball of light quickly turned black. It rattled in the cup of her hands like ball in a bingo cage. The pulsating energy was powerful, too powerful for her to release safely anymore. Mixed with all her love for Jayce and her fear of everything, it extended beyond the knowledge of her education. There was no way of predicting what would happen should she slip and drop this bomb. "Oh heavens! What am I doing?" she cried. "I can't stop it! Someone, help me! *Please*!"

Massive chains of spectral steel exploded from the floor. Twisting around Morgana, they bound her.

"*No*! The spell!"

The glowing ball bounced off her fingertips. It touched the floor only for a fraction of a second before shrinking to the size of a peanut and then ballooning into melon of blistering sun plasma.

"The spell!" Sotomayor warned. Chains contained the ball before it managed to fill the room but not before it burned a pit revealing the floor below. The roof was also on fire.

The quick action of the staff kept the school from being reduced to rubble. In the Room of Detention, a normally impenetrable box sealed by the strongest magic contained Morgana's body. Beside her, her spell rattled the chains of another box because there was nowhere safe on the continent to dispel it.

Morgana's coffin occasionally failed to contain her fits of rage and grief. Devastating rays of emotional magic shot out and bounced around the room like laser beams. School psychologists said that her consciousness was like a muddled pond, unable to see clearly and lost until the debris settled. She may have broken away from reality when crushed with the reality of her failures. Yet, her prognosis was good and she was expected to make a full recovery in only a few days' time.

Sotomayor convened a conference of province leaders to determine what to do with her. There was little agreement, but two camps eventually emerged. The governor of the Land of Rock was prepared to cast aside Morgana, his own citizen, to execute an abundance of caution. If she lacked any natural ability to control her powers, and the most talented school on the continent failed to teach her, then Morgana could not be saved. She should be excommunicated from the college and banned from ever using magic again.

Sotomayor, awash in guilt, argued for mercy. She warned that if they did not intervene with a caring, focused approach soon, Morgana Benevolent may grow into a threat for her home province and possibly to the entire continent of the Rock Gods. Sequestering had the potential to only allow her challenges to fester and intensify.

The vote cemented a bleak future for the Land of Rock.

Two weeks later, Morgana was banished from the Boston College of Magic. She accepted this merciful punishment in exchange for immunity for the damage and injuries she inflicted.

She packed her bags and traveled far away into the heart of the continent. Shame, regret, and hopelessness made homes in her heart. She wondered what future someone like her could still have. With Jayce, she had a difficult life ahead of her. But alone?

Exhausted, dirty, and barely caring enough to eat a single bite, she stopped at a diner near the border of the Pop Populous and Synth Kingdom. While waiting for a plate of eggs and licorice, she stared blankly at the children's place mat on the table before her. A word search caught her eye. She found the name 'Jayce' written within it. It was not one of the listed words. Did she still have a chance for a serendipitous ending?

She grabbed a crayon and began listing all of the most powerful healing spells she knew. She racked her brain over what could possibly keep the fire within Jayce at bay. She flipped the placement over for more room but found a map of the continent instead. Her eyes were naturally drawn to the blazing Mount Rock of her home province. It occurred to her that perhaps she did not need to find a specific spell, but instead just needed the overwhelming strength to overpower her inner demons.

Deep within the college library's forbidden tome dungeon, she once read of a place of immense power. This demonic site could still hold hope for Jayce. Yet, no wizard or witch had ever pinpointed the exact location because of its surrounding environment. With no future ahead of her and a past she desperately wished to forget, she committed to discovering this longshot.

She knew the secret lay somewhere inside a volcano she grew up not too far from. How she would somehow explore it successfully where countless others had failed, she was unsure.

Begin Ocean Avenue by Yellowcard

VERSE 1

There's ... night.

Morgana climbed mountainside of Mount Rock, the tallest volcano in all the provinces. On her way to the summit, she incinerated mountain trolls, dispelled bandits, and cast cooling spells on herself to protect her from the sweltering lava flowing down from the crater.

Stepping triumphantly upon the peak, she peered down in awe of a molten lake of fire. The legends teased that the power to grant one magical wish laid within the crater. Yet none had ever survived the search.

With some courage, but mostly sadness and a lack of will to live, Morgana threw herself into the giant maw. The seething wind licked her face and hair. Her wizarding robes began to burn away and left a rainbow of colored smoke in her wake. She hastily cast a cooling spell and engulfed her body in crystal of blue ice much like the one that imprisoned her beloved.

As the lava rose up to take her, her life began flashing before her eyes. She saw the years of abuse, disappointment, and broken promises. But then she saw her years at school and how it was made right by her love for Jayce.

CHORUS

If ... yeah!

Their first year, Jayce fought off those bullies who tormented her for not being able to play an instrument. She was forever grateful for Jayce's kind heart.

Their second year, he handed her the medal that inducted her into the magical society for the gifted. This unlocked her path toward the best magical opportunities.

Their third year, he helped her learn the xylophone. She finally learned to rock like everyone else.

VERSE 2

There's ... tonight.

Her body splashed down into the searing ocean. She heard the surface of her magical barrier crackling. She had nowhere near the barrier skill of the headmistress. Realizing her mistake, she twisted herself around to swim back out, but she saw only lava. She had already begun to sink too fast.

Her heart was filling with a kaleidoscope of emotions. What if Jayce woke up on his own at any moment? She may never be there if he finally did.

CHORUS

If ... yeah!

She closed her eyes as she began to feel the overwhelming heat seep into her shell. She made her peace and prepared to greet the afterlife when lava caved in and surprised her. There was no burn upon her skin, only an equally warm sensation emanating from within her. Her curse, chaotic fire within her heart, matched the ferocity of the planet's hottest element. She was protected by a bubble of pure smoldering emotion. She descended slowly into the heart of the molten underworld.

INSTRUMENTAL

♫ ♫ ♫

After some time, the glowing red darkness around her began to break. She noticed a white light from below creeping up toward her. She slipped through the surface of a still lake of magma. She ascended into the air and floated through a vast cavern, bright and pleasantly warm.

BRIDGE

I ... somehow.

She hovered toward a stony island and landed softly. A mild breeze blew through her hair. She noticed an altar at her feet.

She knelt and read the inscription upon its ancient surface.

Ye who place thine indomitable hands upon this slab shall be granted the true yearning inside thine heart.

She quickly slapped her palms onto the wedge and laid bare her wish to keep Jayce safe. In her mind, all she thought about was curing Jayce. But the slab did not care for the wishes of the mind. It only promised the truth within one's heart. Its' piercing gaze saw the cause for all her dreams: the power to conquer fear.

CHORUS

If ... yeah!

The volcano erupted, spewing molten rocks across the continent and launching a bright star into the ashen sky. High above the Continent of the Jam Gods, a new goddess was born. Morgana Malevolent received the overwhelming and frightening power to crush all those she feared, the very power she yearned for her whole life. As she surveyed the land, her heart was filled with ambition.

With her mind befuddled within a quagmire of opportunity, desire, and revenge, it was strange that Jayce did not make an appearance within it. But that would all change in the years to come after she shaped the Land of Rock into her own personal empire. Safe, obedient, and finally afraid of *her*.

End Ocean Avenue by Yellowcard

9 *Candii, Candles, and Cuteness*

"Can you hear me? Are you okay?"

Candii opened her blurry eyes and saw a lanky basement troll leaning over her. Was this a continuation of the weird dream she just had? She could barely remember it, but she remembered the emotions she felt: fear and rage.

"No, no," she said in a stupor. "I don't want to go out with you. Get a job and take a bath."

"What? Rude." Krawl let Candii be and tried to wake up Sir Taco.

Candii's mind became clear and she sat up. She was in the van and it was running and warm. Krawl had repaired it and was now trying to attend to everyone's needs.

"How long have we been out?" she asked.

"Hard to say," Krawl said. "The fact that you're all still alive means probably not long."

She was wrapped in a warm blanket covered in Krawl's Killer Solo's logo. The others had snow boots and hats that looked the same.

Krawl finally woke the others. "So, next time you all try to take a detour to the freezing tundra, bring some warmer clothes. You're lucky I had a few pieces of promotional gear left over from the last time I flew out here."

Sir Taco smiled. "Yeah, we didn't really think this one through. This is a pretty dangerous area, huh?"

Krawl nodded. "Every year, a lot of people freeze out here when they get caught in totally metal snowstorms. It didn't always used to be a snow tundra like this. This used to be a desert. A pretty mild one, too."

"What caused hell to essentially freeze over?" Key asked.

"A few years back, the desert elves failed to impress Queen Morgana and so now they live in perpetual snow."

"Elves? How cute!"

"Also, you're lucky the winds weren't absolutely nuts today or I wouldn't have been able to get out here so fast in the Rock-o-copter."

"Did you just call your helicopter a rock-o-something?" Thad chortled.

"Hey, don't judge. That jammin' vehicle just saved your butts."

Thad smiled. "You're right. Thanks for the rescue. So, uh, what do we owe you for this?" He groped under his seat for the sack of cash he brought with him. "I know you don't take mainland bills, but we're willing to give you double the fee. Consider it payment for the cost of getting them converted."

"Oh, I almost forgot to tell you, I already took the sack of bills."

"What!" Key said. "That's like a hundred thousand dollars! And I thought you didn't even take that mainland money!"

"Your buddy is right. Enough of an administrative fee makes this the same as Continent Cash. Also, my bill is rather high. Consider that I'm also just taking some of what you still owe me for the rental."

Key was at a loss for words but could not argue with the price of saving their four lives.

Krawl departed via copter and blasted absolutely metal tunes out of loudspeakers dangling below.

Just as he flew far enough away that the low hum of the blowing wind returned a sense of calm to the van, Candi shouted inappropriately loud.

"Okay!"

Everyone jumped.

"What's the matter?" Key asked.

Candii stared straight out the windshield with white knuckles wringing the steering wheel. "So. We all had a near-death experience, I don't want to talk about it, so I'm going to put the pedal to the metal and get us to that pearl that'll help make everything better! Here we go!"

She accelerated and swerved wildly onto the road. They approached the lake with haste.

"How much father?" she asked.

"We're coming up pretty quick!" Thad said.

"But how far until I gotta..."

"Stop!"

The worn tires skidded along and off the icy road. The van slipped just a touch onto ice. A thin crack gave way allowing the lake to take a bite out of the left tire.

Candii swore as the van tilted. After no further rocking, she kicked open her door and stomped out.

Key poked her head out. "What happened? Should we be abandoning ship, Captain?"

"No, it's okay. Tire just fell in a tad. This shore is shallow. But..." She gazed upon the otherwise white and azure glistening solid frozen surface. "I'm afraid the rest of the lake..."

Thad smiled. "Given the circumstances, I only take slight pleasure in saying I told you so. On the bright side, I have almost exact coordinates of the pearl. It should be about fifty paces directly ahead."

Candii shielded her eyes attempting to search the lake. The blinding white of the tundra made it difficult.

Sir Taco hoped out and scanned the ice with his dark shades. "The pearl lodged itself in the center under the ice. I can see its glow. I'm going out there."

Candii grabbed his hand. "It's too dangerous! What if you fall through? Isn't freezing once already enough? There has to be a safer way!"

Thad opened the van door and threw out layers of fabric. He tied jackets, long-sleeved shirts, and thin blankets together.

"Here, tie this around his waist."

Candii wrapped the end of the towline around Sir Taco.

Sir Taco took a running start and leapt onto the ice penguin-style. He slid far toward the center of the lake and clawed at the ice.

"Too fast! Slow me down!"

Candii, Thad, and Key tugged at the line.

The line tightened with a snap. Sir Taco stuck his arms and legs out spreading his weight over the largest area.

"Good! Good! I'm just about right over the pearl." He plunged his arm into a narrow hole of freezing water. Feeling the top of the pearl, he stretched just a little more and grasped it in his palm. "Got it! Reel me in!"

A thunderous crack extended from the icy hole all the way back to the shore. Growing pressure demanded a release. Water sprayed into the sky from the fissure.

It reminded Candii of a memory as clear as glass. It was like lava from an erupting volcano but she had never seen a volcano in-person.

Inside her mind, the memory took a murky form. It was not her own but an echo from her earlier dream.

As disturbed as she was, Thad and Key screaming to pull, pull, pull brought her back to the present.

"Come on! Run, run!" Thad yelled.

Sir Taco stumbled to his feet and slid just ahead of the growing crevasse that was splitting the ice sheet in half. Plumes of bone-chilling jets shot out at his feet. One large eruption startled him and the pearl leapt out of his hands.

"Someone, catch!"

Candii thew down the line and slid onto the ice with unsteady balance. The pearl fell into her cupped hands just as Sir Taco zoomed past her and grabbed her arm. They collided into the shore's soft snow. The lake completed its split into two. Dual ice sheets splashed against the shores narrowly missing the band.

Candii dug herself and Sir Taco out of the snow. She looked at the pearl in her hand. "This one is for Rainbow."

They packed back into the van and drove off farther west toward the second unicorn pearl of the tundra.

Deep into the frozen wasteland, the band came across a small village of about ten igloos. Colored string lights, candy cane street sign poles, and little smoking chimneys clued the band in that the village was populated.

"How quaint!" Key squealed. "It's like a little Santa's Wonderland!"

"I didn't think people could actually live inside igloos. Aren't they just one room?" Candii asked.

"Yeah," Sir Taco said. "It wouldn't be my cup of tea to have my bathroom in my bedroom."

Thad pointed toward a set of igloos. "Park over there. We'll be close." Once stopped, he checked the signal again. "It's definitely here. If I had to guess, I'd say it's inside the igloo on the right."

The band stepped out onto the frozen little street and pointed out small mailboxes in front of the igloos. They approached the target igloo and Candii had to kneel to knock on the small wood door. She heard shuffling inside. Then the door opened.

"Hello?" To everyone's surprise, a little elf popped his head out.

"You are SO cute!" Key cried. She reached out and squeezed the poor elf's cheeks. They were rosy red and absolutely as soft as taffy.

Candii slapped Key away and bowed embarrassingly at the elf. "I'm so sorry. My friend has a thing for cute stuff. My name is Candii. Please excuse me if I'm coming across rude, but I'm here to ask if you have a shiny ball inside your house."

The elf rubbed his tiny cheeks and smiled. "Oh! You must be referring to my new mood-lighting bulb. Are you the manufacturer? Wow! What great customer service!"

Candii was not following. "Mood-lighting bulb? No, this is a round orb that emits light and warmth. It's about the size of a softball."

"Yes, exactly," the elf said. "We have it inside. While I appreciate the same-day delivery, I have to say I find the product to not quite meet the specifications advertised online as you no doubt read in my email. I expected it to be shaped like a candle and I thought it would emit more heat than it does. Maybe it's defective? If you'd like to come inside and take a look at it…"

"Yes, please," Candii said.

The elf opened his door and made way for the band to squeeze inside. "The name's Weeoo. Welcome to my humble abode." He shook each of their hands as they entered. Inside, the band was surprised to find the igloo empty.

Sir Taco looked around and wondered if anyone was really living here. "Where's all your furniture?"

"What? Why, in my house of course." Weeoo waved his hands shooing Sir Taco a few steps back. Then he dusted off some snow from the ground and revealed a trap door. He lifted the door and gestured everyone to follow him down a well-lit staircase.

Candii descended below and was astonished by a fully furnished multi-room home under the ice. Another elf sat at the dinner table.

"Lyla, the customer service reps are already here!"

"Oooweeooo, Weeoo! You sent that email like ten minutes ago!"

"I know!"

Candii did not want her unintentional farce to go on any longer, so she attempted to correct them. "It's nice to meet you, Ms. Lyla. I believe there may be some misunderstanding. We're not a repair service. We're the rock band The Non-Traditional Key Gullz. We're just looking for unicorn pearls. They're softball sized glowing orbs that fell from the sky recently."

Weeoo looked puzzled. "Oh, so you're not from Jungle Shopping? What are unicorn pearls?"

"I told you, Weeoo," Lyla rolled her eyes. "There was something weird about that mood-lighting bulb. For goodness sake, it was smoking in a crater on our front doorstep."

"Oh, I thought that was just because of the same-day delivery speed."

Lyla shook her head with a tender smile. "Just give the nice people the pearl or whatever. They seem like nice folks and it is their thing."

Weeoo walked into his kitchen. Candii spotted the unicorn pearl sitting in the center of their kitchen table. It emitted a miraculous glow that painted the walls like stars in the night sky. It was so romantic. Weeoo handed the pearl to Candii.

She held the pearl close to her chest. "This one is for Twinkle," Candii purred as she felt comforted by the pearl's warmth.

The band thanked Weeoo and Lyla for their kindness and were on their way up the staircase when Weeoo let out a big sigh. It sounded too big for his little body. "I'm sorry, Lyla. I thought date night was going to be more romantic, but now we don't have any soft mood lighting for the house."

"That's okay, honey. Thank you for cooking dinner." Lyla gave Weeoo a little kiss.

"Oh my gawd. That is SO cute!" Key said. She melted off the staircase and formed a puddle of strewn about limbs on the floor.

Candii tried not to step in Key and shot determined glances at the band. They nodded back.

"Weeoo," she said, "thank you for giving me the pearl. You have no idea how thankful I am and how important this is. I think the band and I would like to thank you for your kindness, if you'd like to accept."

"I don't know what you mean. That is yours after all. There are no thanks necessary."

Candii waved away his words. "As I said before, we're a band. Several of us believe in the power of restorative justice and we can't just ruin your date night without trying to fix it. If you'd like, we could play for you and your wife to help set a romantic mood for your date night."

Lyla clapped. "That would be very kind of you! If you don't mind, we'd love to hear your music."

Sir Taco and Thad ran to the van and retrieved their instruments. Candii and Key sat with the elves in the living room.

"So," Candii asked, "what kind of music do you two like?"

"He likes alternative," Lyla said.

"And she's a little bit country," Weeoo said. "Normally folks wouldn't think the likes of us two would get along, but she and I have always known we were the ones for each other."

The two rubbed their noses together.

Key slapped Candii's thigh repeatedly almost being reduced to a giggling mess.

Lyla took Weeoo's little hand. "I thank the Jam Gods every day for him. He's perfect and I could not ask for more."

Candii thought for a moment and then said, "I think I have the perfect song. If you'd like, we can play while you eat dinner."

Begin I Could Not Ask for More by Edwin McCain

INTRODUCTION & VERSE 1

Lying ... face.

Sir Taco lit candles on the kitchen table. Thad loaded their plates and poured their drinks. Key tapped slowly on the drums, a departure from her usual breakneck speed.

Weeoo smiled and took a bite of his dinner while staring into Lyla's eyes.

PRE-CHORUS

These ... more.

Candii strummed her bass at a sleepy-slow pace, but a love song was needed in this moment.

Lyla laughed when Weeoo missed his mouth with his drink and she dabbed his shirt with her napkin. Lyla shared a story about when they first met. The band learned Weeoo and Lyla met at the desert oasis trading post, both unsuccessfully trying to sell umbrellas as a part of a multi-level marketing job.

VERSE 2

Looking ... me.

Weeoo recalled their first date and how he had replicated that same meal for this night.

Lyla was impressed by his memory.

Weeoo pointed out that their first date's chicken was technically Thai and they were eating Chinese flavored chicken tonight, but he was unable to find Thai spices in town.

She said that was perfectly okay.

PRE-CHORUS

These ... more.

Thad poured Weeoo another glass of wine before he was even finished with his first. Weeoo downed it and asked for another; it was his favorite.

The elves spooned mashed potatoes into each other's mouth.

Key struggled to keep playing because she was overcome by elf cuteness.

Sir Taco dug around in his pocket and found some votive candles. He lit them around the kitchen.

CHORUS

I ... me.

Sir Taco kept digging in his pockets and found a beautiful ring. He slipped it into Weeoo's hands under the table. Weeoo tried to graciously deny the gift but Sir Taco insisted.

Weeoo presented it to Lyla who was overwhelmed with gratitude. They gave each other a great big elf hug and the room audibly sighed.

Candii dug around her pockets and found mostly lint and Tias nacho-flavored corn chips. Further down she found a pack of gum and a bottle opener. Having nothing else to give, Candii slipped the bottle opener under the table to Lyla.

Lyla accepted and presented it to Weeoo.

PRE-CHORUS

These ... more.

Weeoo noticed it was engraved with the logo of the rock band Paramore. He explained how it was his favorite band and that it was incredibly thoughtful of Lyla to give such a gift.

Thad brought the pair a bottle of champagne and Weeoo got to use his new bottle opener.

"Oh! It's so bubbly!" Weeoo giggled as it tickled his tiny, rosy button nose.

CHORUS x2

I … more.

Noticing that the two had eaten a lot of garlic, Candii offered her pocket gum to the couple. They chewed up and were minty fresh.

Thad swooped in and bussed away their plates.

Sir Taco began washing the dishes and cleaning the table with his non-microphoned hand and the couple took their leave into the living room.

With all the chores complete, the band wrapped up their show and thanked Weeoo again for his kindness.

"Thank you for a wonderful night and for truly setting the mood right. You may not be from Jungle Shopping, but you have impeccable customer service!"

End I Could Not Ask for More by Edwin McCain

The band said their goodbyes and packed back into the van to leave the frozen tundra for good.

10 A Declaration of Love in Song

On the road again, Thad directed the band toward a local community college on the western side of the Land of Rock.

"I'm so glad we're out of that snowy wasteland," Candii said. She slipped out of her Killer Solo branded winter wear and back into her old crop top and hot pants.

"It wasn't all bad," Key said, changing as well. "I don't want to ever forget the world's cutest couple!"

"Let's not forget our near-death experience. I vote we never go back," Sir Taco said.

The band agreed to avoid the tundra like a plague and shared the stories of what they dreamed about during their ice-induced death sleeps. Candii was last to go.

"So, what glittery, rainbow-infested, magic eye dreamland did you end up wading through," Sir Taco asked her.

"I...I..." The dream that had haunted her earlier was now a hazy memory so ill-defined that she no longer could understand it. "I don't remember but I definitely dreamed of something."

"Something good, I hope," Thad said. "Feel free to take another go at it, everyone. We're still a few hours from our next stop." He waved his hands as if gripping a steering wheel. "Want me to take the reins for a tad so you can get some much-earned rest?"

Candii saw that he too was quite tired. "No, I'm all right," she smiled. "Enjoy a nap for me and just be ready for whatever's next."

"Roger that." He leaned back in his seat and started a soft snore.

The late afternoon sun cast a beautiful orange hue over Bro-cha-cho Community College as Candii drove slowly through the center of campus. She pointed out that every student had an acoustic guitar. Scores of bros serenaded starry-eyed peers in the soft grass underneath a canopy of bushy trees.

"You know," Thad said, "I expected to see a few acoustic guitars on any college campus with romanticized students swooning over the musician's mediocre skills, but this is a little overboard."

Sir Taco rolled down his window and made a hand dolphin to surf on the wind and chill tunes. "Yeah, but I guess this is what you'd expect on a continent built on music."

The band could not resist visiting the college's bookstore before resuming the search. Comfy collegiate sweatshirts and novelty shot glasses called to them.

Key held a tee shirt in her hands. "Candii, look at this!"

Candii looked at the shirt but could not read what was written on it. "Is that upside down?" While the shirt was right side up, she tilted her head until she read, *IF YOU CAN READ THIS THEN I'M TOO DRUNK. PLZ PICK ME UP.*

On the other side of the store, Sir Taco was carrying a handful of rocking school-branded goods and his sight was completely obstructed. He tried to watch where he was going but he collided into a student.

"Ope!" A female student fell to the floor and swag rained down upon them.

Sir Taco frantically began picking up all the items and offered a helping hand to her. "Sorry! I got lost in all the stuff I was carrying and wasn't watching where I was going."

"Oh, no. It's my fault. I had my head in the clouds," she said with a warm smile. She stood up with his help. Her big, round glasses were tilted to the side and her glittery sweater was all twisted.

"Hi. My name's Sir Taco. Again, my apologies regardless."

"I'm Mary Sue." She straightened her glasses and smoothed out her sweater. "Is that your real name?"

"Um, well no, but I can't honestly remember my real name. So Sir Taco is good enough for me," he laughed.

"Okay." Mary Sue seemed distracted. She searched the floor and picked up a little card. Then she sighed very loudly.

"Are you okay?"

"Oh, it's nothing. I was going to buy this card but now it's all crumpled from the fall."

Sir Taco saw the greeting card in her hand. "Oh. Then let me grab you another one. Where are they?" He began searching the racks around them.

She very dramatically sighed again. "It was the last one they had. I needed that particular one."

"I'm sorry. Maybe I can help you pick a new one?" he asked with cards overflowing out of his hands.

Mary Sue threw her hands up with exasperation. "I can't just get *any* card. I needed that specific one. It had the message I needed." She shook her head. "You see, I got this glowing pearl and I was going to give it as a gift with the card that said, 'You're my *Earl* of Nottingham'. I was going to scribble a little 'P' in front of Earl and it was going to be this whole pun thing. Get it?"

Sir Taco shook his head.

Mary Sue continued unfazed. "It's just boy trouble. Don't worry yourself about it. It's my problem."

Sir Taco was happy to stumble upon the pearl, but he could not just take it from her and leave her in this rut. He considered that the band's recent problem-solving track record was pretty good and he did ruin her boy bait by being careless, so he resolved to try to help her first and then ask for the unicorn pearl later.

"Hold on for a second!" Sir Taco hustled around the bookstore until he got the band together. "Listen. I found the pearl but I also blew the candle out on an innocent youngster. I want to help this Mary Sue solve her boy problems in exchange for the pearl. Fair and square."

The band agreed no one deserves to be boy blocked. They found Mary Sue and Candii offered their help.

"We'd like to help you get your man if you'd be willing to give us that pearl you found," Candii said.

"And what are the rest of your names? King Chalupa and Royal Icing?"

"Huh?"

"Never mind that," Sir Taco said. "We're a band and we can help you deliver whatever message you want. You don't need the card anymore."

Mary Sue bobbed her head energetically as she considered their offer. "Okay. I guess I don't have anything to lose. Without the card, the pearl is pretty useless."

The band high fived and decided to get to know Mary Sue and her future husband. The fact was, she said, they were already married and he just did not know it.

Mary Sue bought the band meals in the school cafeteria and she explained to Candii that she was in love with her class representative president.

"He's so dreamy and strong and brave. He keeps everyone organized and tells everyone what to do." She clasped her hands over her heart, looked up, and swooned in her chair. "I like that part the most!"

Candii nodded. "I can see where you're coming from. So, what have you tried so far?"

Mary Sue thought hard. "Well, I tried sharing with him that we have all the same interests. We both like video games, particularly the Tales of Melda on the Pretendo 64, so sometimes we talk about that. I was in the same bowling class as him and I'm a very avid bowler so I showed him my skills."

"Oh, so he asked to see you bowl?"

"Uh, not exactly. I just tried to do really well whenever I noticed he was looking in my direction. Oh!" She perked up. "I am *also* a class representative so I get to see him every week at the meeting. I try to get on the same committees with him."

"Okay. It sounds like you've been trying. What seems to be the problem then?"

Mary Sue threw herself onto the table and buried her face in her sweater. "Oh, Candii! He doesn't notice me! He probably thinks of me as just a friend!" She sobbed ever so slightly.

"Ah, so you're having trouble painting him the picture of your relationship together," Sir Taco said with his mouth full of enchiladas. "Don't worry, everyone. I think I have the answer for our problem."

"You do?" Mary Sue lifted her head off the table and hope shone through her watery eyes.

"Yep. A musical declaration of love!"

Within the hour, Mary Sue stood outside of Steppenwolf Hall holding a sign and dressed in her Sunday best.

Begin Fantasy by Mariah Carey

INSTRUMENTAL

♫ ♫ ♫

"Are you sure this is going to work?" Mary Sue asked. "Why am I wearing my fancy clothes?"

"You need to paint the picture of what he's missing!" Sir Taco said.

Key nodded. "We need to stop beating around the bush and instead hit him over the head with a hammer!"

Sir Taco stood next to Mary Sue with his microphone in hand. "I'm gonna hand you this mic and you're going to start singing the verses. The band and I will join you on the mic during the chorus parts so don't be spooked when we pull in on you."

"I'm so nervous! I haven't sung in front of other people since grade school choir!"

Sir Taco gave her a reassuring pat on the back. "Do you remember the lyrics?"

"Yep. I'm very good at remembering things."

Candii came tumbling out of the Steppenwolf front doors. "Oh schnitzel! Here he comes!" She ran toward the band and picked up her bass.

Sir Taco tossed Mary Sue the microphone. "Play time is over, Mary Sue! It's time to belt your heart out!"

VERSE 1

Oh ... mind.

As the boy walked outside, Mary Sue sang. The boy was caught quite off guard by the musical display, but he saw Mary Sue's sign with her distinctive handwriting propped at her feet. The sign read, 'I can be your Melda'.

CHORUS

But ... baby.

The band joined in the chorus. The loud display attracted the attention of a nearby crowd. Mary Sue was sweating profusely. During the chorus, she took a moment to compose herself.

"Am I doing it right?" she asked Sir Taco.

"You're doing amazing! Where did you get that voice?"

"I don't know! I haven't practiced in years!"

Sir Taco laughed. "Share it with the world! Sing out loud and proud!"

VERSE 2

Images ... again!

Mary Sue hardened her grip on the microphone and took slow steps toward the boy as she sang. He was visibly intrigued and started to tap his foot.

"You got him!" Key said. "Now go in for the kill!"

CHORUS x2

But ... baby.

The band nudged forward and provided her with musical support from behind. The crowd around them began to dance and clap. Mary Sue felt the energy in the crowd and began to sway from side to side. The boy picked up on the vibe and began to match her count.

Mary Sue was startled when she ran out of slack on the microphone chord. Sir Taco ran along the chord and untangled some of the knots. It gave her enough room to keep moving forward. Inch by inch she closed the gap between her and the boy.

Key sighed. "Ah, young love."

Thad nodded. "They say you're more likely to find the love of your life during your college years."

"Does that mean more than half of these students are in love?"

"Based on the amount of grooving right now? Probably!"

Mary Sue took another step forward but stepped on her dress. She ripped a tear in it and tripped forward, tangled in the loose fabric. Candii leapt forward and pulled on the fabric. It ripped cleanly away. Mary Sue tumbled forward and into the boy's arms wearing a new avant-garde skirt.

"Oh!" he exclaimed warmly.

BRIDGE

I'm ... sleeping.

Mary Sue sang in his arms, unfazed by her clumsiness and filled with confidence by the band.

CHORUS x2

Oh ... baby.

The band continued playing as the boy and Mary Sue slowly sat on the ground as if they were alone on the lawn. The party around them really began to pick up as the street started to overflow with dancing students. The band reeled themselves in and surrounded the couple to keep up the illusion that the two of them were alone.

"I didn't know you felt this way," the boy said.

"It's just my sweet, sweet fantasy. That's all," Mary Sue replied.

After the crowd dispersed, Mary Sue ran inside and brought out the unicorn pearl. "Thank you so much! I think it worked!" she said as she glanced behind and saw the boy still watching her.

"I think it did, too!" Sir Taco said. "Best of luck to you both."

Sir Taco handed Candii the pearl. She held it close to her heart and felt its owner whisper to her. "This one is for Dazzle."

The band headed further into campus to find the second collegiate pearl.

End Fantasy by Mariah Carey

11 Crashing the Party and Crashing the Crashers

Shad referenced a campus map and led the band to a visitor's center. Candii approached a student receptionist sitting at an information kiosk with a worried expression. He asked her about the pearl.

"A meteor-like glowing pearl?" the student asked. "Yeah, I know what you're talking about. There are a couple of those floating around campus."

Candii laughed as she slapped her knee in relief. "Wow! I'm so glad this was simple. I was sure you weren't going to know what I was talking about."

"It was a pretty big deal and everyone was talking about it. One crashed into the clock tower the other day and the Party Planning Committee plucked it out."

Candii smiled from ear to ear. "Where is it now? Can we have it?"

"Of course not! We're using it as a disco ball for the school dance that was supposed to be tonight."

Candii's smile did not break. She nodded patiently and said, "Okay. Well, how about after the dance?"

The student thought for a second. "I don't see why not. I'm on the planning committee so I can just ask to give it to you when we're done. I can't imagine what else we'd use it for, but it is saving us hundreds of dollars versus buying a professional disco ball."

Candii clasped her hands together. "Excellent! This is still the easiest pearl we've recovered yet. So, when can we pick it up? I suppose we could use a little rest and relaxation and enjoy your beautiful campus for just a bit until tonight."

"Tonight? The dance has been delayed. We were supposed to have the dance tonight, but Queen Morgana blew up the guest band because they changed their sound on their latest album. We got a couple feelers out there, but we probably won't be able to sign a contract with a new band until next week. I don't know. Maybe if we could find a band faster, then we could hand it over sooner. But I don't know where we're going to find someone so last minute."

"A whole week?" Candii cried. "We can't wait a whole week…"

Key grabbed Candii's shoulder. She spun Candii around and rolled her eyes.

"What? What is it?"

The band gave her stone-faced glances. Key pointed to her. Then she pointed at herself. Then she pointed at Thad and Sir Taco.

"Oh!" Candii shouted. She turned back around and pounded her fist on the desk. "Kid, you ever hear of The Non-Traditional Key Gullz?"

"OMG! Like, my roommate, Becky, the one with the good hair, and I love classic NTKG. Why? Do you know them?"

Begin Wonderwall by Oasis

INTRODUCTION & VERSE 1

Today … now.

The band agreed to play for the college's school dance after dinner. After a simple setup and sound test, the show was ready to begin. Hundreds of students crowded into the gymnasium and mingled among the flood of locals who were lucky enough to hear the NTKGs were playing.

"Wow, I'm surprised how many people are here for a last-minute concert," Candii said.

"I heard flyers with our name were plastered all over town," Thad said. "I guess word gets around fast."

As the curtains rose, they played the one song they knew every collegiate fan in the room knew by heart.

Students raised lights into the air and sang along. Nowhere else but at a bro school would one-hundred percent of the student body know every single word to Wonderwall.

Candii looked up at the ceiling and saw the unicorn pearl hanging, emitting beautiful blasts of color all over the room. "Listen up, band. Keep our eye on the prize." She strummed her bass and sent good waves reverberating throughout the crowd.

VERSE 2

Backbeat ... now.

Key was bopping her head to the beat when she glanced up momentarily. She was startled to see a shifty shadow walking among the rafters and meddling with the unicorn pearl.

"Hey, look!" she pointed out for the rest of the band.

PRE-CHORUS

And ... how.

"Hey, you! Leave that alone!" Candii tossed her bass guitar to Sir Taco and waved for the crowd to separate below. She hopped down onto the dance floor and ran across the room and beneath the unicorn pearl. The crowd watched with excitement at what the cool Candii of NTKG would do next.

"Shoot!" a crackly voice above said. "Queen Morgana's not going to be pleased if that woman gets in my way."

Candii pushed further through the crowd and found a ladder along the wall that led up to the rafters. The crowd cheered and danced unaware of the gravity of the situation. She climbed to the top and hopped onto a rickety metal catwalk. The attached spotlights swayed about and created a club-like atmosphere down below.

CHORUS

Because ... wonderwall.

"Who the heck are you, buddy?" Candii asked.

"I'm just a humble aspiring servant of the great Queen Morgana. There's a bounty out for these glowing pearls. Why ask questions when the pay is good?"

"Because I'm probably going to kick your gnarly behind?"

"I think I'll take my chances," he snarled. He left the pearl in its chandelier and faced her with his fists out.

VERSE 2

Today ... now.

Candii rushed at the hooligan and tried to tackle him, but he dodged and spun around. He grabbed her shirt and pulled her off balance.

Candii fell on the hard metal but managed to pull herself free. She hopped up and again faced him.

He laughed in jest.

Candii reached into her pocket and the hooligan did the same. She paused dramatically and then whipped out a guitar pick. He whipped out a dagger.

Candii frowned. "Well, this isn't going my way."

PRE-CHORUS

And ... how.

The hooligan took a swipe at Candii's chest, but she backflipped out of reach.

Candii aimed and flicked her guitar pick at the hooligan's face, hitting him in the eye!

"Jeez! Watch the face!" he said as he dropped his weapon. "Oops!"

Candii rushed him and picked him up by his waist. She slammed him down on the platform and sent the whole thing rocking.

Students down below hollered with delight as the two of them scrambled to grab onto anything to prevent them from falling. The hooligan kept cupping his watering eye with one hand and was unable to keep his grip. He slipped and fell in between the crowd below.

"What a rock show flunky. Anyone who has been to enough concerts knows how to fight!"

CHORUS x3

I ... wonderwall.

Candii stayed up top and riled the crowd up with some sick dance moves. The band played the song out and bowed to the crowd. She untied the knot suspending the shining unicorn pearl and slowly lowered it to the band. Sir Taco took it into his hands and waited patiently until Candii descended as well. The band congratulated her and the crowd lifted them all onto their shoulders.

As they were carried outside to the after party, Sir Taco handed Candii the pearl.

She cupped it in her hands. "This one's for Shimmer."

After the crowd put the band down, a group of students threw the hooligan on the ground in front of them.

"Have mercy!" he cried, kneeling before them.

Candii grabbed him by the collar and shook him. "You tell Morgana this: we're *getting* the unicorn pearls and coming for *her* next!" She released him.

The hooligan scrambled to his feet and ran away.

"I think we should have clobbered him into next week!" Sir Taco said. "Why'd you let him go? I doubt Morgana would have been so kind with one of us."

Candii shook her head. "I don't go overboard. I'm not cruel like *her*."

Thad warmed the van's engine. "That puts us at eight pearls," Thad said. "We just need to keep hunting these down and we'll have them all in no time!"

The band hit the road and headed back east toward a large cache of unicorn pearls.

End Wonderwall by Oasis

12 Cruisin' for a Bruisin'

It was getting late and the sun was casting an orange glow over the land. Sir Taco was snoring. Key was awake somewhere in the back tapping her fingers on the window with a smooth rhythm. She was keeping herself sharp.

Candii noticed Thad stuttering awake from a cat nap next to her. He fumbled with his GPS, catching it before it fell out of his hands. Her own eyelids felt heavy as she watched the traffic lines on the highway tunneling past the van. She was tired.

She had driven the entirety of a long day so far. But this was merely a test of endurance, she told herself. She was responsible for bringing everyone else along and a little fatigue would not stop her burdening her friends as little as possible and still saving her unicorns.

Thad saw houses springing up over the horizon followed by tall buildings and skyscrapers covered in a red and black haze. "We're just a few minutes outside of what appears to be a major metropolitan area. It's called New Rock City."

"This looks pretty normal," Key said. "I don't see any robots, ice storms, or chaotic confectionary hiding anywhere."

He nodded. "According to the Land of Rock tourist guide website, this is the province's capital."

"Oh! There must be so much going on here!" Key squealed.

"Yeah, that's right. Apparently, all this action also means a lot of opportunity. My GPS is picking up at least ten unicorn pearls all over the city!"

They drove downtown and saw many people walking, minding their business just like any mainland city. Except for the penchant for clothing to be made of leather and hair to be long and rocking, it was a normal metropolitan downtown.

Candii parked in front of a hotel and the band booked a room. After they checked in and settled down, everyone gathered in the lobby to review the GPS. She wanted to pinpoint the locations of any nearby unicorn pearls that could be grabbed easily before resting for the night.

"I've identified five unicorn pearls in what a tourist map calls the theater district," Thad said. "My guess is we're going to find a bunch of high-powered creative types using the unicorn pearls to flex their creative muscles. Two others are in Boys Town, another in an orphanage, one in a funeral home, and one across the street of this very hotel."

"Those are some tough places to rock out in," Sir Taco said. "And I thought playing Devil Went Down to Georgia at a bar mitzvah was hard."

Candii nodded sleepily and hid a yawn with her hand. "You're right. We'll do our best to be respectful while retrieving the pearls."

"Taking a unicorn pearl from an orphanage?" Key muttered, gritting her teeth. "That may be the new 'stealing candy from a baby'."

Candii patted Key's shoulder. "We'll tackle that moral quandary if we find it. Ready to head out, everyone?"

The band affirmed, but Key placed a hand on Candii's back. "Are you sure you want to do this tonight? We could just take the night to recover and hit them up tomorrow."

Candii shook her head. "There's no telling whether these pearls will be gone tomorrow. We need to keep up with Morgana no matter what. We've already made great progress."

"Right!" Key nodded.

They headed toward the van. They were surprised to find the van had been robbed of its tires. It now sat on cement blocks.

"Wow! Maybe this *is* just a normal city and not some weird alternate rock version!" Key said.

Thad called Krawl at the van rental place and began working out a solution while Sir Taco paced around the block with Candii.

"I just don't want to deal with this right now," Candii fumed. "Every moment we spend dawdling is another second Morgana may find the misfired pearls before us. We're also all out of cash except..." She dug a couple hundred out of her pocket. This was food money.

Sir Taco found a twenty-dollar bill and a button in his jeans. "I wouldn't be surprised if this was Morgana's doing. She has henchmen all over it seems."

"Her highness sends her regards! Ha, ha, ha!" A truck sped past full of hooligans waving the van's tires above their heads. Candii noticed the distinctive glow of a single unicorn pearl coming from the truck's bed. She surmised it was the very one they detected across the street. The hooligans were probably watching them the whole time.

"We've got to catch them!" she cried. Sir Taco followed her as she chased them around the next corner, but they couldn't keep up on foot. Thad and Key came up behind them.

"What were you chasing?" Key asked.

Out of breath and hunched over, Candii cursed. "Tia chips and ranch dips! That truck has our tires and a unicorn pearl! We gotta get new wheels fast to chase them and…"

Candii turned back toward Key but she was no longer paying attention. She was staring at a billboard.

Candii stepped next to her to see too. "No. No, no, no, no, no. There is no way you're getting me onto one of those!"

Begin Downtown by Macklemore

INSTRUMENTAL

♪ ♫ ♫

The band wandered into a moped lot designed for tourists and day trippers.

"Listen up, folks. Let me do the talking," Thad offered.

"Wow, the prices are really low. We could afford a set of daily rentals," Key said.

"These salesmen can be really tricky. Don't worry, though. I'm going to haggle really hard and get us a good deal. Remember, never accept the first offer!"

Key checked a price tag. "But we can actually afford these…"

"Never accept the first offer!" Thad repeated sternly.

VERSE 1

I … deal!

Thad spoke to the first salesman he saw and was dazzled by the moped floor models. He accepted the first offer.

They signed their temporary driver permits, took the keys, and jumped onto the bikes.

VERSE 2

I'm ... Dope.

The band burned rubber out of the parking lot with matching cute blue helmets covered in yellow stars. They cruised after the moving dot on Thad's GPS.

"They're a few streets down at a stop light!" he yelled back to the band.

The GPS dot was nearing so they approached slowly and tried to stay inconspicuous. They cruised in pairs with Thad and Candii leading the way, and Sir Taco and Key hanging back. They stopped at an excruciatingly long stoplight.

VERSE 3

Killing ... player!

The light turned green and they darted in and out of traffic with grace and speed.

"We're not far now!" Thad shouted as he consulted his GPS.

"Let's pick up speed! I see the truck ahead!" Candii said. "I'm going to blast them to pieces!"

They each put their pedals to the metal and weaved through the cars like a needle through thread. They were only a few cars behind the truck when one of the hooligans casually glanced back and caught sight of Candii. He immediately recognized the fury in her eyes.

"Fiddle sticks, boys! We got big trouble! Hit the gas!"

The truck lurched forward and blew the next red light. It narrowly dodged the cross traffic. The band took advantage of the stopped vehicles and followed in pursuit without slowing down. Cars filled with musical instruments beeped musical jingles warning them of their dangerous driving.

Candii's intense focus upon the unicorn pearl ahead aided her delicate driving skills. A pothole up ahead caused the rest of the band to change lanes, but Candii accelerated and jumped the hole, pulling ahead of the others and leading the pack.

PRE-CHORUS

Downtown ... legs!

Loud ringing bells from a temple's stone tower rang a rock-like tune; something no one thought was possible from classical bells.

Even though the chase was dangerous, Sir Taco's distracted mind took a moment to admire the beautiful city. Large stone arches up above indicated a city built at the turn of the century. Holiday decorations for the next big celebration hung from the light posts proclaiming 'New Rock City' proudly.

The band began to approach the truck and the hooligans took notice again.

CHORUS

Downtown ... Downtown!

"Boss!" one shouted from the truck bed to the driver. "We gotta do something quick! She's gaining!"

The driver shouted back. "Use the glowy magic ball! Rub it on the truck!"

The hooligan followed orders and the truck began to handle smoother and gain some speed. The wheels rubbed against the concrete and sent rainbow sparks flying behind them.

Fiery steel and asphalt brushed Candii's face. The shower grew too intense and she had to fall back to keep her moped steady.

"Yeah, that's it, boys!" laughed the driver. "We'll lose them easily now! All hail Queen Morgana!"

"All hail the Queen!" they shouted in chorus.

VERSE 4

Dope ... suit.

The rest of the band caught up to Candii.

"Hold onto your seats!" she yelled back. "We're about to go into orbit!" The road ahead was becoming hilly and curvy. Everyone screamed as they soared over the tops of hills and gripped their handlebars tightly.

Key's wheels fell onto the road hard and she swerved a little. "Woah! I almost lost control!"

"We need to finish this fast before it gets more dangerous," Candii said.

A series of green lights kept the chase high speed. The truck bucked wildly up and down the hills. The hooligans hollered as they desperately tried to hold on to the truck bed.

"Oi, mate! Don't launch us all out of here! Watch what you're doing, you dumbass!" said one.

"Let me see what I can do," the driver called back.

The truck took a sharp turn and lost some speed as it tried to stabilize down a flat and straight street. The band followed and pushed their little moped engines to the limit as they caught up to the truck. Thad and Candii pulled up along opposite sides of the truck.

"Pull over, you mother truckin' ding bats!" Candii said. She made a cutting motion on her throat. "I've had a very long day and I am in *no* mood for this!"

"We can do this the easy way or the hard way!" Thad said bumping his moped against the truck's door.

The driver scoffed. "People from the continent are hardcore. You can't intimidate me!"

Candii tipped her head back to Sir Taco and Key.

The duo pulled behind the truck's bumper. Stacks of amps were strapped to the front of the mopeds. A flurry of switch flipping hummed their plan to life. Sir Taco whipped out his microphone. He set the moped on cruise control and leaned forward with one foot balancing on the handlebars.

"Boss!" one of the hooligans shouted. "They got amps! Huge amps!"

Key twisted the knob of her amp. "How high?"

"Let's take it to the limit!" Sir Taco replied, the static hum of his own set growing stressfully stronger.

She nodded and spun her control up to 10.5 into the yellow danger zone.

Sir Taco belted into the microphone and undulating waves of visual distortion washed over the truck.

PRE-CHORUS

Downtown ... legs!

The truck began to shudder and sway. Nuts and bolts became loose and littered the street.

"Boss! We're losing hardware!" the truck bed hooligans yelled. "What's the plan?"

The driver growled. "We were ordered to stall like our lives depended on it! I'm starting to think we're dead no matter what! Either these has-beens get us or Queen Morgana will!"

A tire popped off the truck and its front smashed into the road. Bearing down on the asphalt, fireworks began spraying over the hood and onto everyone. The driver could not see anymore and he gripped the steering wheel with white knuckles as he spun out wildly and crashed into a lamp pole. The band pulled up beside the truck and Sir Taco continued to roar majestically into the microphone.

CHORUS

Downtown ... Downtown!

The hooligans covered their ears and fled into the alleyways nearby. Glowing definitely inside the wreckage of what little of the truck remained, Candii found the unicorn pearl.

"Holy tortellini, what a rush!" Key laughed as she skipped off her slowing moped and joined Candii's side.

"This unicorn pearl is for Glitter," Candii said. She held the pearl close. A warm, healing aura filled her with hope.

Sir Taco plucked the stolen tires out of the debris. "One tire per person. Chop, chop, ya'll. Let's get back to the van, pronto!"

After returning the van to its former glory, they were once again scouring the city streets for the remaining urban pearls.

End Downtown by Macklemore

13 A Tell-Tale Pearl

Candii pushed her foot to the floor, jolting the van forward, and sleepily drove the band into the theater district.

"Woah!" Sir Taco said. "That's a bit of an iron foot, don't you think?"

She eased off the gas. "Sorry! I think I zoned out there for a second."

He reached to unlatch his seatbelt. "How about you pull over and we switch…"

"…no! I got this. You should rest, okay? You haven't gotten any sleep in a while."

"Neither have you."

"I…I just need to be strong enough for them."

"For whom?" Key poked her head into the front.

"My equestrian team. If I can't push it to the limit when it really is *all on the line*…" She squeezed the tar out of the steering wheel. "…do I really deserve them?"

Sir Taco nodded slowly. "Okay…just keep your eye on the road, please."

They drove among the blinking marquee lights and fashionable thespians walking the streets. The nightlife was just coming alive and the night was young. As they rounded a corner, Key spotted a surprising sight.

"Look! It's the witch!" she said. Morgana floated out of a second story window with a glowing unicorn pearl in her hand.

The sorceress noticed them and raised an annoyed eyebrow. "I didn't think you'd be so capable at finding these powerful gems scattered all over my kingdom. Because of your little road trip, you've forced me to get my hands dirty. You should know that my New Year's resolution was to get out of the house more, but I can't say I appreciate it."

Morgana floated amid the rooftops like a scarf in the wind. "I have four unicorn pearls with me now. That should be enough to begin my work. I've run out of patience with this particular one inside, though. The man is not responding to pain and I don't have the time to handle him with a more delicate approach."

"You dum-dum!" Key shouted. "You're going to leave it here for us?"

Morgana chortled. "Hardly. From what little I know of your boring band, you're only good at beating sound into skulls. I doubt you have the nuance to manage this matter." She wrapped herself inside her cape. "I grow tired with your yapping. I'll return another time and further cement my power." She vanished into thin air.

"Four gone? Ugh!" Candii yelled. She slapped the steering wheel repeatedly. "We were too late!" Dizziness descended upon her. "Whoa." She held her head.

"Are you okay?" Key asked. Key placed a hand on Candii's shoulder. "It sounds like she's done for the night. We can pick this up again tomorrow morning, bright and early, and beat her back to this last one."

"No..." Candii murmured. "The unicorns are in pain. I can feel it." She placed her hand on her heart. Tiny emotional strings, stretching across the land, sea, and air, connected her with her team back home. As time went on, the unicorns neighed more slowly. Their will was draining and whatever residual magic was left in them was waning as well. If she failed to restore their magic soon, they would revert to horses and lose all their talents and intelligence with no hope of restoration. "We must press on."

"Then there's no time to dawdle." Sir Taco said. "Let's get inside and make this quick."

The cramped three-story brick flats that lined the sidewalk from corner to corner were still alive with activity. Windows leaked out warm and cool glows both and the sound of entertainment was clearly audible. However, one apartment separated itself from the rest. A bleak white light passed through the open window that the sorceress had used. One could sense that there was no happiness inside.

The band climbed the flat's stairs and gently knocked upon the apartment's door. It swayed open gently so Sir Taco poked his head inside. He was wowed by beautiful artwork on enormous canvases filling the otherwise barely furnished studio. Despite the brilliance of the artist, the paintings seemed sad, adorned with tortured figures in reds, blacks, and grays. "Clearly a starving artist lives here," he said.

"And his name is Pablo." A man emerged from behind one of the paintings. His threw his hand dramatically over his forehead. His pose candi sad face identically matched the painting. It was kind of funny in a sad clown sort of way. "Have you too come to criticize me?"

"What? No." Candii stepped forward. "Is that what she did to you? That witch who was just here?"

"She's right, you know. I'm an untalented hack. I'll never break out of depressionist art." Pablo sighed and slumped to the ground. He fingered a paintbrush and smeared a blue teardrop down his cheek. "I'm a one-trick pony."

"Yikes. That's a little harsh, don't you think? I'm sure..." Candii looked around the room. She only saw sadness. "...you're good... at other stuff... too." She looked to Key for support but she only shrugged.

Pablo moaned. "Noooo...it is not my talent that is in question! No, it is my ability to break out of my artist's block! I can't explain it but ever since a shiny ball flew through my window, I've been bombarded with ideas for the depressionist art I was experimenting on."

"A pearl?" Candii asked, leaning forward.

"Oh? You're here for it too?" His head tilted. "I told Morgana and I'll say the same to you: I hate the thing but I'm going to try to make some money off of it so I can pay for therapy. It's clear that it certainly has value. I'm going to keep it a little while longer until I can get it appraised. I don't want to get swindled."

"Rats." Candii had half a mind to just take this man by the arms and shake him until he gave up the pearl's whereabouts, but Morgana already said force did not work. No, she would need to do this in a non-traditional way.

"The muses keep coming and they won't stop coming," Pablo continued. "My feet hit the ground and my brush won't stop running. I'm so over this style but I feel compelled to keep pouring out more depressionist art."

"Have you tried drawing a happy little flower on any of these?" Key examined a particularly gloomy piece of a stone gorge filled with deflated red kick balls. "Maybe just plant a really bright one right up here. Right up in that little crack," she pointed upon the canvas.

Pablo sighed again. It went on for far too long. "Oooooh, I am a man driven by my emotions! Maybe if I could be inspired by some other powerful emotion, then I could evolve past this passe style and finally reinvent myself. Yet, I literally feel trapped within depression. Why can't I seem to shake this all-encompassing state?" He rolled across the wooden floor like a pencil and stopped below a series of small canvases all sporting his face in different colored boxes. He slumped onto his feet and drew his face close until he was aligned with one of the portrait boxes. He was now a part of the piece. It was a very interesting performative art.

Thad called the band together in a huddle. "So I did a quick internet search and looked up all of the symptoms he described. As an amateur internet doctor I'm thinking the unicorn pearl is giving Pablo this amazing amplification of his muse and skill. Yet somehow it's got him stuck in it as well."

"But how can we help him move on?" Candii asked. "I'd suggest giving him the therapy he needs but none of us are qualified to do that."

"Yeah," Thad sighed. "Web doctoring can only get you so far."

"Well, he said it himself. Didn't he?" Key asked. "It's the emotion that he's stuck to. So let's move him with some other emotion."

Key broke the huddle and turned to Pablo. "What are you feeling inside?"

"I am lonely, dear stranger."

"Why are you lonely? Where are your friends?"

"They abandoned me. They said I would only hold them back because depressionist art is so last week. Now they're all into angry art. Pfft. That'll never take off." He slowly turned to the side and whispered, "I refuse to admit that I'm jealous."

Key turned back to the band. "Get the instruments!"

Begin Boulevard of Broken Dreams by Green Day

VERSE 1 & 2

I ... walk.

"Hear our words, Pablo," Sir Taco said as he pointed at him. The band played their instruments and began to find their rhythm.

Pablo cracked a smile and pointed at himself. "Who, me?" The happy curl of his lips did not last. His mouth curled back down as if pulled by the gravity of the Earth. "What is wrong with me?"

"This song is dedicated to all your lousy friends." Candii shouted. "We're going to direct your feelings in another direction. Now do me a favor and imagine those suckers for me."

Pablo closed his eyes and tried to envision his bad friends who ditched him; it made him feel mad but then sad. He saw only darkness and shadows. He could barely remember their faces.

CHORUS

My ... alone.

The same mysterious force filled the room and kept drawing his thoughts back to depressing things. He felt the urge to keep painting right then and there. He brought out a blank canvas and splashed what appeared to be random colors of paint across it. The oils dripped from the canvas and formed puddles staining the floor. What remained was just one big crying face.

"Wow, he's good," Candii admired. "Although he's still stuck in his rut."

"Do your friends have names, Pablo?" Thad asked.

VERSE 3 & 4

I'm … alone.

"Yes. There was Janus, Peter, Pauley, and…" Pablo stopped and sat still for a moment. "…and Johnny."

"Who is Johnny?" Thad asked.

"Oh, he was just my best friend, but I don't know anymore."

"Why? What happened?"

"He abandoned me." Pablo picked up a small picture frame with a picture of him and Johnny. They were holding hands and frolicking in the park. "Just when I was hitting my stride this week, he stopped supporting me."

"Some friend he turned out to be," Sir Taco said.

CHORUS

My … alone.

"Actually, Johnny seemed to be a *very good* friend," Key winked, whispering among the band. "That would make me very sad too, Pablo."

"Breaking up with someone can definitely lead to intense sadness," Sir Taco replied. "Combine that with emotional magic and you're in for a roller coaster."

"This is the work of the unicorn pearl," Candii said. "It seems messing with one's emotions can be an unforeseen consequence when granting greatness. I wonder what other unpredictable effects the unicorn pearls are having on their users."

"Hey, Pablo!" Sir Taco shouted. "If Johnny was really your boy, he wouldn't have left you in a lurch!"

Pablo had not thought of or called Johnny in days. He thought maybe he was wrong for not reaching out. But then again, if Johnny really wanted to talk, *he* could have picked up the phone.

INSTRUMENTAL

♫ ♫ ♫

Pablo remembered Johnny instructing him to call when 'he got good again' before walking out the door one last time. Tears streaming down his face dried up.

"Johnny, you said we'd be together forever. You said you believed in me. That was a lie!"

"Now we're getting somewhere. We should hire out our services as musical therapy professionals," Key joked.

"Wait!" Candii scolded. "He's going in the wrong direction! We gotta reroute him towards acceptance."

VERSE 5

I ... alone.

Pablo squeezed the handle of his paint brush with purpose. He approached a canvas of a beautiful man surrounded by thorns and spikes. In one fell swoop, he added a set of angry eyebrows on the man. It was jarring. It was madness.

"Was Johnny ever on my side? Was he just riding my coattails?" He splashed paint across the floor. "They all were!" He threw himself down and rolled around in the puddles. Greens, golds, grapes splashed across the apartment. Candii jumped back to avoid a splattering upon her legs.

Sir Taco shielded his face from the splotches. "No need to get too crazy, my dude. You can always learn to forgive..."

"No forgiveness!" Pablo yelled. "I'm so mad!"

Key tapped Sir Taco on the shoulder. "Maybe anger is just as good as any emotion?"

Candii shook her head. "I don't like doing it this way, but we're running out of steam."

CHORUS

My ... alone.

"Yeah, Johnny sounds like a real jerk..." Sir Taco said.

Pablo jumped around the room drawing angry eyebrows on all of his work. Some of the fresh paint continued to drip and created unibrows and mustaches on the figures.

"I think you've found your next muse," Thad said.

Pablo gazed upon his modifications. A wry smile spread across his face. "I think you're right, stranger!" He skipped into the center of the room and pried open a floorboard. A white beam shot out as he pulled a glowing unicorn pearl from inside. "Here, take it! I don't need it anymore. I've moved on to hate-art!"

Candii clutched the unicorn pearl with unease. "This...this one is for Princess."

The band stepped into the stairwell as Pablo paid them little mind, a paintbrush in hand and shouts of maniacal laughter filling the apartment.

"Are we sure it's all right to leave him here like this?" Candii asked.

Thad scratched his head. "I'm pretty sure once we get this pearl far enough away from him, its lockdown effects will wear off and he'll be back to his previously 'normal' self."

They loaded themselves back into the van.

"Okay, but when this is all over, we have to come back and check in on him." Candii safely stored the unicorn pearl in the back with the others.

End Boulevard of Broken Dreams by Green Day

14 Under Pressure to Break the Wall

Our next pearl is located somewhere in the office building district," Thad said, consulting with his GPS.

"Off-isis…office buildings?" Key muttered, unfamiliar. She placed an inquisitive finger on her chin. "An office. "Now, isn't that where people go to get a job that sucks out their soul?"

Sir Taco shuddered. "Why would anyone not live for the music, man?"

"I don't have any more 'real-world' job experience than the rest of you, but I believe that's right," Thad said. "While we should be careful to not get sweet-talked into six-figure paychecks, fancy titles, and retirement accounts, we need to dive in and find the unicorn pearl. Keep your guard up."

Candii's wavering eyes navigated the streets of the soul-crushing district. She felt more exhausted than she expected to be after the last short show. Perhaps she unintentionally overexerted herself? No, that did not make sense. She knew herself and her limits. Something else was amiss, she was so sure of it.

To keep herself awake, she scanned the buildings for anything interesting, but this worked against her because every storefront looked the same: gray and square. Unamused people marched in many straight lines on their way to work. They all wore gray suits, holding briefcases, and sporting sad haircuts filed in lines along the sidewalks.

"It's almost the middle of the night! How are there still people going to work?" Sir Taco asked. "I'm happy staying as far away from this as possible!"

Thad pointed toward the next intersection. "Take the next left. It seems the pearl is on the move, albeit slowly."

"No car chase? I like that." Candii followed his directions and soon they spotted a man clutching a glowing briefcase. "That's not something you see every day."

Candii pulled the van up next to the man and lowered her window. While slowly following the marching drone's forward pace, she leaned out the window casually and asked, "Hey. What's in the briefcase?"

The man gasped as if unaware of his surroundings. His eyes darted about like he was paranoid. He clutched the briefcase harder and whispered to her, "Are you with management?"

She shook her head. "Nope. I'm Candii. My friends and I are looking for shining unicorn pearls that fell in the city." She let her eyes wander down to the briefcase.

The man looked at the briefcase as well. "You're looking for this aren't you?" He opened the case and an immaculate glow bathed the band. The boring commuters around him took notice and stepped away from him in disgust. He was like a sandbar in a river and all the people were flowing around him like rushing water desperately trying not to touch him. From the case, he revealed the unicorn pearl and showed it to Candii.

"Ever since it crashed through my apartment window and rolled into my kitchen, I've begun to realize that I don't like my job. I barely tolerate it." He stared at the pearl with sullen eyes. "I think it's messing with my mind."

"That sounds terrible," Sir Taco said pushing his head out next to Candii's. Candii tried to push him back inside but he was persistent. "Maybe you should give us the thing and get your mind back to normal."

The man tucked the pearl back into his briefcase. "No way. I think I like what it's doing. I finally see that my job is sucking out my soul. It's just that I don't know what to do about it. I suppose I'd rather be smart and sad than stupid and happy."

Candii grabbed Sir Taco and yanked him back into the van with her. Quietly, she talked among the band. "This guy's in some pretty deep stuff. Maybe there's some way we can help him feel better about his job? Then he won't need the pearl anymore."

Key shook her head. "I don't think that's the best solution. He doesn't seem right for this type of life. We can't just fit a square block in a round hole even if it means getting our hands on it. We gotta help this guy. We should find him a new job."

Candii nodded and leaned back out the window. "Hey man, what's your name?"

"Bob Boberton," the man said.

Sir Taco tugged at Candii's shirt. "Are you sure he isn't meant for this boring life? His name, for crying out loud!"

"Look at his socks!" Key pointed out the window and the band leaned out to stare. Bob wore boring gray shoes and pants, but occasionally, when the city wind blew just right, his socks would poke out. The band could see socks adorned with blood red roses and gnarly razor-sharp thorns. "It matches my shirt!" Key pointed at her rose pattern. "This guy is destined for better things than this!"

"Oh, these?" He lifted his pant leg and flashed those rocking beauties. He said in a low hush, "I find having a bit of personality in my wardrobe helps me stay sane." He approached the van window and whispered even quieter, "But that type of thing is frowned upon by the establishment so I have to keep it low key."

"Key is right," Sir Taco said. "He's a wild man at heart."

Candii pushed everyone back inside the van. "Bob, what if we helped you learn to enjoy your job? There's got to be something about it that you enjoy. Maybe it's whatever first brought you to apply?"

He considered it. "It was just a job. I can't say there is anything really fun about it. I don't know if you can help me."

Candii thought for a moment. "Bob, how about we see what exactly it is that you do? Once we get a feel for it, I'm sure we can shine some light on the positive side of it."

"Sure, I guess it couldn't hurt as long as we keep a low profile. If I don't need this ball anymore, you can have it."

Thad opened the door for Bob to jump in. "Let's get you to work and see what you got!"

Begin Bittersweet Symphony by The Verve

INSTRUMENTAL

♫ ♫ ♫

The band followed Bob's directions and drove into a very boring looking parking garage where all the cars looked the same and parked the same way.

"This is my building. I work on the 137th floor," Bob said.

They walked through the parking garage and boarded an elevator.

Key looked over all the buttons and pressed 137. "What exactly is it that you do here, Bob?"

"I count cuebits."

"What's a cuebit?"

"I don't know, but I sit in front of my computer and when I see a cuebit on the screen, I press a button to count it."

Sir Taco turned to Candii and said quietly, "I don't think I could do that for the rest of my life."

"Well, luckily none of us have to worry about that because we're darn good musicians," Candii said. "We rock on to the fullest."

"I wish I had any talent for art," Bob said. They reached the 137th floor and he showed them to his drab desk.

VERSE 1

Cause ... yeah.

Bob turned on his computer and it displayed a blank screen. "Now we wait."

The band stood and stared at the screen for about ten minutes before the screen displayed the number 1. Bob promptly pressed the enter key. He did not say anything; he just continued to sit and stare at the screen. Another fifteen minutes passed and it happened again. Another three minutes passed when it happened a third time.

"This is it. When I first started, I didn't care about the work. I just liked the paycheck. But now that glowing ball showed me that it's not enough to just work for the weekend. You gotta light up your life with something that you're passionate about."

"And this?" Candii asked.

"Yeah. This ain't it."

CHORUS

No ... no.

Sir Taco pulled at his hair. "We got to get Bob out of here! I feel corporate just by looking at him!"

Key searched Bob's cubicle for anything fun. He had a single stress ball that was just a gray sphere. "Not even a freakin' smiley face printed on this thing? Oh boy! We're in trouble!"

Candii flashed a nervous smile. "So what skills do you have?"

"I've never missed a button press. I'm very detail-oriented," Bob said.

"Do you have any other skills?" Candii asked hopefully.

"No one's ever asked me that."

VERSE 2

Well ... now.

The band followed Bob to the break room. He pressed a button on a beverage machine and it dispensed a gray-colored coffee in a gray cup. "Sometimes I like to come in here and pretend I'm the break room valet."

Thad poured himself a gray cup of joe. "What does that mean?" He took a sip from his cup and gagged.

"I prepare extra coffees and put different flavors in them. I put them out and see what faces people make when they drink them. I make sure the napkins are stocked and sometimes refill the creamer pump."

"Does that excite you?" Sir Taco asked.

"A little."

"And that is not a part of your job?" Candii asked as she sifted through the sugar packet brands.

"Nope. It's just a little something I do to take my mind off work."

CHORUS

No ... no.

"Bob, do you like to take care of others, to organize things?" Candii asked.

Bob stared out the breakroom window out onto the floor of cubicles. "I suppose so. I do enjoy contributing to other's success."

Behind the other two chatting, Key whispered into Thad's ear. "Maybe he'd like to be a retail manager."

"Or an executive assistant," he replied.

Key eyes lit up with a brilliant idea. She threw her arms over Candii's and Bob's shoulders and pulled them in close toward her in the middle. "How about Bob participates in a micro-internship with the world-famous rock band The Non-Traditional Key Gullz?"

"Are you sure that isn't *too* extreme of a leap for..."

"Sure, why not?" Bob replied without a second thought. "Maybe I could do with a little something outside my comfort zone." He looked up at the ceiling. "Or, is that this glowing ball talking?"

VERSE 3

Cause ... yeah.

The band and Bob all took seats in the break room and went over their expenses, trip schedule, and other random clerical considerations. Bob took to it like a fish in water and quickly organized their budget and optimized their route through the city toward the remaining unicorn pearls. He was like a savant with the logistics and he knew so much about New Rock City, such as traffic patterns and neighborhood trends.

"Wow, Bob's a natural!" Sir Taco admired as he slowly nursed a cup of gray coffee that Bob had specially prepared. "This coffee would be ding dangly awful if not for Bob's special touch, too!"

"You really think I have talent? No one's ever said something like that to me," Bob said.

Candii patted his back. "It turns out that you're a born clerical manager. We need to get you out of this button-pushing job and in charge of an office!"

"That sounds nice, but I'm under contract. I can't leave until I die."

Sir Taco spit out his coffee. "What the heck?"

CHORUS

No ... no.

"What happens if you break your contract?" Candii asked.

"Oh, they throw me in a dungeon for the rest of my life. It's all according to an official decree issued by Queen Morgana a few years ago."

Sir Taco threw his cup across the room. "You have got to be kidding me! What if you just want to switch careers?"

"Well, there is one way. If I can get out of the building before my shift ends, I'll be fired and can leave freely."

Sir Taco took Bob's hand. "Okay! Let's get going then!"

Bob shook his head. "But nobody has ever managed that considering security issues a code red whenever one of us wanders off our designated floor. I've seen people dragged screaming back to their desks."

Candii turned to the band and gave them a devious look. "You said next time I was thinking about doing *it*, I should tell you first."

Key jumped out of her chair. "Are you for real? You're thinking about doing *that* again?"

"It's the fastest way down. And I don't think anyone is going to want to follow us."

BRIDGE

It's ... silence.

Bob and the band crashed out of a window from the 137th floor. For a few moments, they flew like birds suspended among shards of glass and the potted plant they threw through the window. The remaining folks in the office gasped.

"Give Candii that unicorn pearl!" Key said as they began their wild descent.

"Darn diddly dang! I've never done anything impulsive or crazy like this before!" Bob fumbled with his briefcase. Once unlatched, papers, along with the unicorn pearl, flew into the sky.

"We just passed the 50th floor and we're running out of airspace! Quick, someone grab it!" Thad said.

Candii swam through the air and snatched the unicorn pearl. With all her heart, she wished for their safety. They were surrounded by a ball of glittery white light.

"We're not slowing down!" Key screamed.

They collided with the sidewalk at breakneck speed, but the ball of light squished and recoiled like gelatin. They launched into the air and bounced off sides of buildings like a pinball out of control.

The band screamed and Sir Taco thought he was going to barf, but eventually they settled down in the middle of a small fountain park. Around them, many first and second floor office building windows were smashed open and workers leapt out onto the street and fled, free from their contracts.

End Bittersweet Symphony by The Verve

Kneeling near a fountain, Candii squeezed the unicorn pearl tightly. "This one is for Glitzy." She brushed a lingering remnant of the unicorn light off her shoulder. It faded into the wind like glitter. She turned to Bob. "So, do you have a better idea of what you're capable of now?"

Bob smiled. "I do. I guess I just never knew I could be anything more than a button pusher, but you showed me I have unexploited talents and, dare I say, a sense of thrill. I think I'm..." He looked up at the sky and struck a bold pose. "I'm going to head into another part of the city and look for a new life!"

"We'll give you a ride!" Candii said. Everyone piled into the van and Candii climbed behind the wheel. "Where to next?"

Thad consulted his GPS. "It's time for a real wild time because now we're headed to Boys Town!"

Key did her best dance while sitting and swung her arms around a little too much. She smacked Sir Taco in the face while saying, "Woo! I've been wanting to dance lately!"

15 Double Feature at the Romp Room

New Rock City's heart of the nightlife pumped out from Boys Town. The neon lights made the street look like a party and the large crowds of happy people they passed in the van uplifted everyone's spirit. The band dropped Bob off at a local temp agency and said their goodbyes.

Thad pointed down the street. "We're almost at the nearest unicorn pearl. I think it'll be inside that club." A glowing, glorious sign hanging off the side of a warehouse marked the way to The Romp Room.

Key stretched herself out in the back seat and yawned. "I was so excited to throw down on the dance floor, but now I'm feeling tired and achy from everything today."

"This has been a really long day," Sir Taco said. "Let's make this quick and get back to the hotel. The stakes are too high for us to keep going into these things half awake."

Candii was nodding off at the wheel. Sir Taco tapped her shoulder and she perked up. "I'm okay, it's okay. Yeah, let's just get in and out and get some sleep. After this, I think I can rest my conscious tonight considering all the other amazing work we've done today."

They parked the van outside the club and filed inside the warehouse. Instantly, the band was overcome with an otherworldly feeling. It was the fever of dance and it infected their hearts.

Key laughed. It sounded odd. "You all do your little detective thing. Something's come over me so come and get me when we're ready to rock!" The magic of the beat pulled her onto the dance floor.

Thad checked his GPS again. His foot was tapping quickly to the beat. "It looks like the unicorn pearl is in the far back of the club. Probably in the manager's office, if my knowledge of club architecture is correct."

Candii noticed security guards at every door and on the balcony on the second floor overlooking the dance floor below. "Security seems pretty tight in here."

Thad nodded and led them to a table to sit while he plotted their covert course through the club.

Candii scanned the room. A rainbow flashing dance floor in the center contained over a hundred clubbers. Neon pink lasers and fog rained down from the ceiling. High above the dance floor, Candii noticed a barely visible silhouette against a glass wall. "Is that one-way glass? Could that be a manager's office?"

"Ah," Thad said, noticing it as well. "I think that clue is the final piece of the puzzle. Okay, follow me." He led Candii and Sir Taco through the sea of dancing people, grabbed Key, and slipped into the back hallway past a very bad security guard.

As a door shut behind them, Candii said, "Finally, I can hear myself think again."

"It's a miracle we got out of there without also being swept up in the music," Sir Taco said. "Did anyone else feel an unnaturally strong urge to dance?"

"Now that you mention it," Thad said, "I did feel like danc-ing and I didn't even like that song."

"Yeah, me too," Candii said uneasily.

"I don't know," Key shrugged. She rolled shoulders left and right. She snapped her fingers and bobbed her head. "I still feel a little bit of the groove monster inside me. I think we just needed a little rest and relaxation and the mood was right."

Sir Taco said sternly, "No, I think something is going on here. Let's keep our wits about us because I have a feeling this has something to do with the unicorn pearl."

The band sneaked through the kitchen where Sir Taco stole a chalupa off a plate, then through a back room with a card table covered with questionable kitchen herbs in small bags. Thad took a wrong turn and they got lost in a basement littered with dirty paper money and glitter all over the dingy floor. After that diversion, they found the Manager's door.

"It's locked!" Candii said annoyed when she tried the door-knob.

"I'll be right back." Sir Taco left and returned with a unicorn pearl from the van. He rubbed it on an electronic panel next to the door and it unlocked. "I had a feeling this door could be opened using an electromagnetic pulse. Luckily, I've learned by watching Candii that the unicorn pearls can grant wishes."

"Good thinking." Candii opened the door and the band hustled upstairs and into a second-floor office. At the top, they saw a tall woman standing in front of a giant window overlook-ing the dance floor. She was dressed in the most luxurious silk robe and a wild poofed up wig. Off the reflection of the glass she peered out of, Candii noticed the woman's makeup was a bit much for her taste, but she could not knock it. She was sure it counted as being hardcore in someone's book and rocking on to the fullest was the best way to live.

The woman spoke but did not turn. "The Non-Traditional Key Gullz. Welcome to The Romp Room. This is my establishment and my name is Queen Vanillish Moneigh. I would never have imagined that the world-famous Non-Traditional Key Gullz would ever go clubbing in my little neck of the woods."

"With all due respect, that's not why we're here, Vanillish," Thad said.

Vanillish spun on her heels and jutted a long, bony finger at him. "That's Queen Vanillish Moneigh to you, short stuff!"

Thad smiled nervously. "My apologies! I just wanted to say that we're here for a shiny unicorn pearl. We're willing to make a deal to make this go quickly and smoothly."

"Oh, you mean *those* pearls?" Vanillish pointed through the window into the club. Hanging from the ceiling was a huge laser light and fog machine apparatus. Sitting at the top on a small silk pillow were two unicorn pearls. "Since those two fell from the sky and into my care, my club has been more popular than ever. I don't question the means to this end, but I do relish in its result."

Candii ran toward the glass and pressed her face and hands against it. The pearls were close. "So, the pearls are making your club popular?"

"Yes." Vanillish peeled Candii off the glass and wiped her face and fingerprints away with visible disgust. "People now seem to lose themselves in the music and they tell their friends about how amazing it feels. That has really drummed up our popularity in the area."

Candii realized this was going to be a tricky one. The pearls were bringing her clear, measurable success and there was really no way to hand over a replacement, nor was it exactly a firm problem they could solve in return. But then she had a creative idea. "How would you like an exclusive show with the world-famous Non-Traditional Key Gullz in exchange for both of them?"

Vanillish's eyebrows went up, up, up. "Hmm…" She thought for a moment. She smiled. "If you can pull off the right set list, it would be an offer I couldn't refuse. I'd be promoting your appearance as an endorsement across the continent for years." She began to pace the room. "Yes, I think we can make a deal, but *only* if the crowd loves it. We'll need at least five…no seven hundred club goers and they'll need to stay the whole time. Otherwise, it may cause more bad publicity than good."

Candii extended her hand and Vanillish hesitantly shook it. Candii was about to release when Vanillish grasped her tight again.

"You know the terms. This is no short order. Are you sure you and your bandmates are up to it? You haven't released a new album in what…decades?"

Sir Taco tapped on Candii's shoulder and whispered in her ear, "Are you sure this is a good idea? We're all exhausted."

"Don't worry, I have a plan," Candii whispered back. She said confidently to Vanillish, "Don't forget who you're talking to, Queen V."

Vanillish sent her staff crying in the street to spread the word of a special one-night show. Leaflets soon clogged the gutters and posters infested the sides of buildings.

Inside, there was only an hour until showtime and the band was desperately trying to set up their equipment on stage in time. Key was still tapping her feet, beating her foot pedal, and sending out a cool beat.

"This weird feeling is starting to wear off, but I can still feel the club's pearl magic giving me good vibes. It's like every song is my favorite song," she said.

"I'm hoping that'll work in our favor," Candii said. She plugged in her guitar. "The unicorn pearls are my plan."

"You're right!" Sir Taco said. "I hadn't thought about that. The deal is sure to go in our favor with the power of the pearls emanating down."

The band finished their sound check. Candii poked her head through the stage curtains and saw the crowd pouring in. She sighed with relief. "Thank goodness. There are easily enough people in here. Now all we have to do is perform any old song."

Key slammed her cymbals. "Right! So it's agreed we're going to get this done with as quick as possible and play rock covers of Twinkle Twinkle Little Star and the ABC song?"

"Yes," Candii yawned. "It literally shouldn't matter what we play with the pearls' magic. I also don't think I could stay awake for a real set."

"Did you really think it would be that easy?" Vanillish stepped out from behind an amp. "Silly girl. I anticipated this type of corner cutting from tourists like yourselves. No self-respecting denizen of the Land of Rock would ever try to pass a children's television special for a true concert. And so, I just had the pearls removed."

Candii jumped through the curtains onto the stage. Indeed the fog-laser apparatus above was two unicorn pearls short. The crowd was lethargic, distracted with their cell phones and idle small talk. Their worst nightmare was materializing. She slipped back inside. "You tick-tock trickster!"

"Now, now. I wouldn't be a very good minion of Queen Morgana if I made this easy, would I?"

Thad struck a discordant tone on his guitar. "Curse you, Vanillish! You meant for us to fail all along!"

Vanillish stepped back with a hand on her chest. "How could you accuse me of that? No, that's simply not true! I still very much have a vested interest in your success. You see, a performance from The Non-Traditional Key Gullz with the help of the unicorn pearls would never translate over well on the home video version and official live companion album recording that I plan on selling long after you're gone. No. You need to really pull out all the stops like the good ole days to give me something I can use. Can't you see it?"

Vanillish waved a slow hand through the air. "A truly amazing show from The Non-Traditional Key Gullz in all the papers. Merchandise cross-tagged with my club's name in every apparel store. This one break could skyrocket my small club much farther than a localized cloud of unicorn pearl magic ever could!" Vanillish nodded vigorously as she envisioned her future. Then she snapped her attention back to the band. "Let me be serious. I know you can do this. I know The Non-Traditional Key Gullz are the best, the most rockin' that ever was and ever will be. I don't care what your reasons are for being here. All I care is to see your magic on stage one last time." She winked at Thad and disappeared into the curtain.

With only minutes before the opening of the show, Thad convened an emergency band huddle. "Okay. So we need a quick change of plans. We have two songs to fill and they really need to one, speak to the crowd, and two, keep us awake. Any suggestions?"

Everyone quietly contemplated for a few moments before Key said, "What about something wild that calls the crowd to just love each other in a passionate fireball of emotions?"

Thad nodded. "I like it. You set the beat and we'll follow."

"I know the perfect way to end it," Candii said. "Let's send out a true message of self-love. The people of this land have been through a lot with Morgana as their ruler. Let's remind them that no matter what, they should find comfort in who they are in their hearts."

Sir Taco patted Candii's back. "This woman's on point. I'm in. Agreed?" The band nodded and took to their instruments.

A loudspeaker crackled to life. The crowd fell silent. "My beautiful people! Thank you for joining us today for the most amazing event to ever grace New Rock City, and possibly the Land of Rock, for years to come! You all know me as your Queen, Vanillish Moneigh and I present to you, for *one night* only, the one, the only, the certainly world-famous, Non-Traditional Key Gullz!"

The crowd erupted. The curtains drew back and the band waved hello.

"Thank you all again for coming out tonight!" Sir Taco yelled into the microphone mustering all his energy left inside him. He felt light-headed for a moment, but he pushed through it. "We have quite the show for you tonight, ah ha!" The crowd excitedly bustled and squirmed in anticipation. Waving limbs and turning heads created a blur. Their chaotic screams echoed in his head as if far away. Every blink was a fight to stay awake and his heart was pounding. He shook his head vigorously and then announced, "For our first song, I encourage you all to find that special someone and hold them close. Or, if you're still looking, find your nearest beautiful neighbor and stare into their eyes!"

Begin Animal by Neon Trees

INSTRUMENTAL & VERSE 1

♫ ♫ ♫ ... tonight.

Sir Taco made love to the microphone and the crowd ate it up. Candii laid down a mean bass line, plucking like a mad woman, and set the tone. Key kept everyone on beat with her foot pedal and simple cymbal taps. Thad kept his fingers ready, hovering just above the fretboard, for his big part during the chorus.

Sir Taco saw more people pouring into the club. The back doors were constantly slapping against the wall as several hundred more people squeezed in. The dance floor filled up and folks were climbing onto the balcony level. He turned to the band to nod encouragingly when he began to worry. Thad was staring absent-mindedly at the ground. Key was playing, but her passion was missing. Were they falling asleep?

"Hit it!" Sir Taco roared.

Thad jolted back to life. He nodded with conviction.

CHORUS

Oh ... tonight.

The crowd jumped to life, bouncing off the walls and moshing up a storm. Crowd surfing was par for the course. From the stage, a wave of emotion rippled through the room back and forth.

This was the right opening song. Sir Taco turned up the volume a tad and refined the treble to focus on the words of the next verse. He gazed up into Vanillish's office. Even through the one-way glass, he saw her glowing eyes watching the band.

He winked in defiance.

VERSE 2

Here … you!

Sir Taco continued to sing sweet nectar into the microphone. Patrons looked into each other's eyes and felt the feeling of love and joy overwhelm them in the fever of the moment. No one could hold back and everyone was ready to release the animals inside on the dance floor.

The band fed off of the energy and felt a second wind swirling within them.

"Let's keep this PG-13! We're in public!" Candii pleaded to the front row. As if becoming embolden by her request for decency, one fan tore his shirt open and roared like a lion.

CHORUS

Oh … tonight.

Upstairs in her office, Vanillish laughed to a ghastly minion at her side. "Wow! This is hundreds of times better than I expected!"

"But Vanillish…"

"That's Queen Vanillish Moneigh to you, minion!"

"Ah yes, my apologies, Queen Vanillish Moneigh. But what will we do if they still want the unicorn pearls?"

"Explain yourself, minion."

BRIDGE

Hush … tonight!

"Well, we can hardly hand over the power of the unicorn pearls after Queen Morgana specifically prohibited us."

"Fool! Do you not think Queen Vanillish Moneigh is not a woman of her word?" Vanillish kicked the minion onto his back and pressed her boot upon his chest. "Get out of my sight! If they earn them, they've earned them!"

Back on stage, the band swung left and right in unison. The crowd imitated the band and began to shake the very foundations of the building. The walls shuddered as they danced. Steel structural beams quivered and sent dangerous ripples through the floor.

CHORUS x4

Oh … tonight.

Sir Taco continued to belt out the tone of a generation. Thad adjusted the sound levels again to account for the crowd of now almost a thousand.

"Look at them go!" Key shouted with delight. A piece of the ceiling crumbled apart and fell onto the stage right in front of her drums.

Candii swung around and spotted the debris. "Uh oh! We may have a safety problem!" She pointed above to the balcony where drywall and bolts began sprinkling onto the crowd.

"Vanillish!" Key cried. "Your club is rocking too hard!"

From her office, Vanillish gasped as she realized the building was rocking itself to pieces. She rushed down and jumped onto the stage as the band finished the song.

End Animal by Neon Trees

"Oh! Ha, ha, ha! What a wonderful performance, isn't that right everyone?" The crowd of now a thousand people roared back and sent Vanillish's wig flying. "Oh my goodness!" The band giggled and Thad handed Vanillish her wig.

"Thank you, you handsome boy." Vanillish put herself back together and tried to address the crowd seriously. "Listen up, everyone. I have an announcement to make. It appears we are very much several hundred people over our capacity of this building. I have a warehouse next door made just for such an occasion. Please, can all our people on the balcony slowly file out and follow the direction of our bouncers to the warehouse? I think you will find the neon light display, giant projection TVs, and our open bar to be more than satisfactory."

The crowd did not wait for Vanillish to finish. Once they heard open bar, the building emptied to about half, safely within the limit.

"They're all yours. Can you keep it up?"

"That's what she said!" Key shouted with fists covering her mouth.

Vanillish smirked. "*Right.* You know, if you four didn't rock that last song as hard as you did, I'd agree with the old adage that you should never meet your heroes. But in this instance, I'm willing to see this all the way through and reserve my judgement until then." She walked off stage.

Thad turned to Candii. "You ready?" His vision began to blur as his adrenaline from the last song began to wane.

Candii darted over and steadied him. "Are you?"

"I...I-I just need a second." Thad handed his guitar to Candii and he sat on an amp.

Sir Taco lifted the microphone and said nervously to the crowd, "Just a moment! We want to give everyone next door enough time to settle in and grab a drink! Aren't we considerate?" The roar of the crowd seemed to not appreciate his intention. "Come on, TP! You got to get back on your feet!"

"Get up and play or I'm going to murder you!" Key screamed.

Knowing that she was only half kidding, Thad jumped to his feet and grabbed his guitar. "I'm ready!"

"Calm down, everyone!" Candii said. "We have our limits. I'm worried about us. How are we going to pull through this?"

"What other choice do we have?" Sir Taco asked.

Candii's mind was a fog of sleepiness. Novel ideas were hard to formulate. Yet, one managed to emerge that immediately cleared her senses. "What about we switch instruments? We need some serious mental stimulation and playing what we're comfortable with is only lulling us further into complacency."

Sir Taco nodded. "We do all know how to play every one of these bad boys." He took Thad's lead guitar.

Key handed Candii her drumsticks. "I know you like the drums, but don't get too cozy."

Thad took the microphone. "I mostly just like to sing in the shower. I hope the crowd doesn't judge me."

With a tap of the cymbals, Candii felt her brain tingling at the challenge. "Let's go! I'm going to lead the way, so everyone try and keep up!"

Begin Born This Way by Lady Gaga

INTRODUCTION & INSTRUMENTAL
It ... ♫ ♫ ♫

Key led the band into a pop song wonderland with a bassline that echoed through both venues.

Meanwhile, on the other side of the Land of Rock, Morgana efficiently collected more rogue unicorn pearls. With magical prowess, she flew into the heart of the land's volcano and pulled one out of the magma.

"Ah, a smoky hot pearl of pure power."

She crossed the border barely into the Death Province and entered the catacombs of the dead. She blasted hordes of skeleton armies away and pulled a unicorn pearl out of the crushed skull of a dead queen sitting atop a throne of guitars.

A dying skeleton reached a bony hand in defiance toward her.

"Stop it. It's not like she's going to be able to use it anyway." She smashed its skull in.

VERSE 1

My ... say!

The Romp Room's crowd cheered. They loved the song. The building next door began to bounce and roar with excitement, aided by a waterfall of free-flowing drinks.

In the manager's office, a minion questioned, "Master, are we sure we can afford to give so much free beverage away tonight?"

"People will never stop talking about this show," Vanillish beamed. "The royalties alone in merchandising will be never-ending!" She smiled from ear to ear. She knew this would be a night to remember.

"Master, is the video okay?" another minion recording the performance asked.

CHORUS

I'm ... queen.

"Yes! It's excellent! Be sure to capture the true essence of the audio."

"What does that mean, Master?"

Vanillish huffed and stomped over to the minions recording station. "Give me that!" She adjusted the volume knobs and zoomed in on the band. She shifted the camera past each member.

Thad was belting like a banshee. Sir Taco had his eyes closed in concentration. Key's hands moved like a blur. Candii...there was something strange happening with her. It was as if she was exuding an aura of pure rock essence. As far as Vanillish could tell, it appeared to be raising the general energy level in the club. But she only knew of one other entity that had such potent power.

Meanwhile, on the other side of the Land of Rock...

VERSE 2

Give ... yah!

Morgana handed a rare-collections vendor a burlap satchel in return for the unicorn pearls he recently stumbled upon.

The vendor eagerly counted the gems inside. "I hope you did not find my hardline deal disagreeable, my Queen. I must turn a profit and these are the rarest elements in all the land." He held the gems up to the moonlight and admired their shine.

"I am your Queen no longer," Morgana scowled. She cast a spell and turned the vendor to stone. She took back her satchel of sentimental volcanic gems and then took to the sky, soaring away toward the bustling city of Rockopolis.

CHORUS

I'm ... way!

As she descended between skyscrapers, the Mayors of the Land of Rock's largest cities met her on a dark, hazy street and handed her a box full of unicorn pearls they helped collect.

"You've all done well," Morgana praised. "This will ensure a little healthy insurance."

"Of course, my Queen!" one Mayor said with a bow. "I think I speak for all of us when I say the unicorn pearls are probably best in your hands rather than benefiting our fair cities," he said with considerable snark.

Morgana raised an eyebrow. "Probably?"

The Mayor fumbled. "Oh…m…m-my Queen, I misspoke! I meant to say absolutely! My sincerest apologies!"

Morgana glared at the group before slowly revealing a coy smile. "You are forgiven for your grave transgression."

He bowed again. "Thank you for your kindness, my Queen!"

"Oops. I misspoke. My sincerest apologies." She laughed. They all cried. She cackled hysterically as her hand reached toward the twinkling night sky. All the stars in the heavens seemed to dim as she formed an enormous fireball. With a careless flick of her wrist, she cast damnation down onto one of the continent's most populous cities.

BRIDGE 1

Don't … way!

Vanillish zoomed the camera in on Candii. Candii pounded the drums and sent waves of percussion rattling the bones of all the concert goers. "Minion! Look at this! Do my eyes deceive me?"

"Is she…glowing, Master?"

Vanillish thrust the camera into her minion's hands. "Keep recording!"

She rushed to her safe where she had locked away the unicorn pearls. She swung it open and coughed profusely as a cloud of black smoke wafted out.

BRIDGE 2

No ... brave!

After fanning it all away, she found a red-hot seething hole in the back wall. "The unicorn pearls are gone! They're being drawn to her!" she cried.

On stage, Sir Taco gave a wink to Key who threw the wink to Thad who then sent the wink to Candii. She smiled and diverted her attention above the crowd. She was attracted to a surprising glow.

"Wow!" she said.

CHORUS & CODA

I'm ... way!

Descending slowly from above the dance floor, the two shining unicorn pearls swirled in locked orbit around each other.

Candii grabbed her guitar from Key and threw it into the crowd. The mass swarmed below her and held up the guitar allowing her to leap into the air and onto it like a surfboard. She crowd-surfed her way to the middle of the dance floor where she grabbed the pair of pearls.

"These are for Spirit and Starlight!" she said with relief.

Meanwhile, Morgana sat on her throne inside her massive castle at the top of Mount Rock. She turned a single unicorn pearl in her hand and admired its glow. "You're beautiful...so powerful...so misunderstood."

She glanced at her altar where the rest of the unicorn pearls lay arranged in a circle. They channeled their magic into a hovering crystalline structure above them. "Just like me. Born this way." She squeezed the pearl with anger. "Will you grant me the power to finally end my nightmare?"

Noticing a change in the pearl's shade, she gasped and released her grip. She was losing control over her emotions again. No, not now. Not when she was so close.

"My Queen," a minion interrupted. "I think it would…be best if we carefully leave the pearls safely to their task. Would you like me to return that pearl with the rest?"

Morgana handed the pearl to the minion. "Yes, please. These fourteen unicorn pearls should be treated with care." She closed her eyes and sighed deeply. "Respect, love, and care. These are the joys all things are owed. And when they are mistreated, well, I already know what wrath karma can wrought."

End Born This Way by Lady Gaga

Vanillish emerged from the curtains on stage and patted Key on the back. "You've presented a phenomenal show tonight, far past any expectations I had!"

"You wanted The Non-Traditional Key Gullz so you got it," Key smiled with exhaustion written all over her body.

Candii surfed her way back and hopped off her guitar and onto the stage. She stumbled slightly and regained her balance. "I am beat! Please tell me we're even now."

Vanillish nodded satisfyingly accompanied with a slow clap.

Thad held a calculator and his GPS side by side. "That puts us at thirteen unicorn pearls and there are still this many to go…" He calculated. "What's this? A bunch of the unicorn pearls have been collected into one place!"

The band gathered around him and looked at his GPS.

"Could Morgana have collected that many so fast?" Sir Taco asked. "Last I counted, she had maybe five, tops."

Thad strained to look closely at his GPS screen. "I see fourteen unicorn pearls at the top of Mount Rock, one at the mountain's base, and one in a green city at the northern most tip of this province."

"Did I hear you mention Mount Rock?" Vanillish interjected. She pinched Thad's cheek. "Oh, honey. That's Queen Morgana's lair. You might as well count those as lost."

"Hold on," Candii said. "Our thirteen plus Morgana's fourteen plus the remaining two only add up to twenty-nine. Where's the last unicorn pearl?"

Thad scoured his GPS. "I don't know. I don't see it anywhere in the Land of Rock, let alone the entire Continent of the Jam Gods."

Key was nursing a bottle of water. She stared at the splashing contents. "Maybe it got launched way too far into the ocean."

"Possibly. We'll figure that out later," Candii grumbled. "At least that means Morgana doesn't have it. If we can score these last two unicorn pearls, we'll be one pearl more powerful than her."

"I already told you, honey. Forget about even facing the Queen. It doesn't matter what kind of firepower you're bringing, she's a goddess of magic, emotion, and rock."

Candii clutched her pair of unicorn pearls harder and said with conviction, "Nothing will stop me from reclaiming all of my team's magic!"

Vanillish shook her head and shrugged. She asked the group to follow her and led them back to her managerial office. Everyone took a seat and she turned on a projector. On the wall she presented a map of the Land of Rock.

"Now, as a lover of rock and all that is holy, I suppose if anyone were to ever take down Queen Morgana it would have to be The Non-Traditional Key Gullz. To even have a chance, you would need to traverse a hidden entrance that only her most loyal officers know about. Thanks to the popularity of the clubs of yours truly, I've overheard my share of secrets and know exactly where it is. Anyone crazy enough to attempt it would drive all the way around to the backside of her mountain and access a small mountain road to the sanctum's summit."

"Paha!" Key blurted. Everyone looked at her. "What? I cannot be the only one who saw what she did there! Backside? Small, secret? Sanctum, people, sanctum!"

"This is no joke, I'm afraid. It's a dangerous situation, but the back entrance is the only unguarded way in."

"Bah!" Key laughed. Everyone turned again. "Come on! Are you people blind to comedy?"

"I thought you hated poop jokes," Sir Taco said.

Key nodded. "Yeah, I do. But I'm freaking exhausted and I'm feeling a little delirious."

Thad shook his head. "This sounds great and all, but why should we trust you? You serve the enemy."

Vanillish smiled and walked over to a cabinet behind her grand desk. "Yes, true. I see your point. I suppose I haven't entirely revealed myself to you. Here, take a look at my inner shrine."

"Woah!" Thad jumped back. "I don't mean to be rude, but I don't think we need to know you that well, Vanillish!"

"It's Queen Vanillish Moneigh! And don't flatter yourself, handsome. No, look at this!"

Vanillish opened the cabinet to reveal a collection of The Non-Traditional Key Gullz albums and merchandise. All the greatest pieces were there, like their gold-foiled first-edition albums and limited-edition tour shirts featuring their one-time mascot the

Peanut Grim Reaper. "I'm a true fan. I want to help you in some small way, but to be honest, I still think you have no chance."

"Thanks, Queen Vanillish Moneigh. I think we'll take our chances." Thad waved for the band to follow him out, but then paused for a second. "What's going to happen to you for helping us?"

Vanillish chuckled. "Don't worry about me, handsome. Survivors like us, we always find a way to thrive."

Assured that Vanillish could take care of herself, the band returned to the van. Thad saw that the nearest unicorn pearl was in a very green part of the Land of Rock known as The Pantry, where all the farm fresh food for the Land of Rock came from. They packed their equipment, signed a bunch of autographs, and left New Rock City. The night had mostly escaped them so there was no reason to stay at the hotel. They would drive through the remainder of darkness and sleep in shifts.

16 A Recipe for Confrontation

Sir Taco volunteered for the second driving shift with Key refreshed and awake as his co-pilot in the back. Thad napped in the front passenger's seat and Candii slept sprawled out like a starfish in the back. The early hours of the morning covered the road in mist and darkness.

"That show really seemed to wear her out," Key mentioned as she held Candii's head in her lap.

Sir Taco nodded. "Yeah. I think she took it a lot harder than the rest of us. I still think we should have stayed the night in the hotel even if it meant sleeping into the daylight."

"She wouldn't have it. The shock of those fourteen pearls already being in Morgana's hands really shook her." Key stared out the window. A volcano on the horizon erupted for a moment and sent fireballs into the sky. "Candii's been expending an exceedingly high amount of empathy during our battles. I can just feel it in my heart. While it's wearing her thin, I don't think we could've done it without her."

"Well goodness knows I'm not very empathetic. So more power to her, I say."

"If that's true," Key said, "then we may find ourselves at a disadvantage if she becomes exhausted during a song or, knock on wood, something were to happen to her..."

"Nothing will happen to Candii. We came here to help her and that's what we're gonna do," Sir Taco said sternly.

It was obvious the band had entered the outskirts of The Pantry because the black and gray landscape of the volcanic Land of Rock turned to lush green vegetation and fields of golden wheat. Thad's online research told them that this specific region fed the people and was an incredibly popular tourist spot for its denizens who wished to indulge in a scarce commodity in this province: tranquility. The Pantry also had a very strong foodie culture that focused on culinary connoisseurs and craft creations.

"The GPS has the next unicorn pearl about twenty minutes away," Thad said, awake and refreshed from the nap. "There appears to be a city there, but I'm having trouble reading its name on this tiny screen." As they approached, he pointed at a large welcome sign. "Metal City: Home of Metal Stadium."

"Oh, that's fun!" Key giggled. "Maybe we can catch a sports ball game while we're in town. See them throw the sports ball, catch the sports ball, score the sports ball. That's how sports work, right?"

The van approached a large stadium in the center of Metal City. Spotlights cut through the thick volcanic clouds that occasionally wafted into the area from the neighboring volcano.

"This appears to be the place," Thad said. "Yes, the unicorn pearl is somewhere in that stadium. Let's pull into the parking lot."

"Okay, I'll try to find a spot." Sir Taco entered the large lot and drove up and down the aisles for what seemed like a lifetime before finally finding one space far in the back.

"Oh boy barnacles! Hauling our equipment all the way to the entrance is going to be a slog. Where exactly is the entrance?" Key asked as she unpacked their instruments.

Newly revitalized Candii poked her bedhead out of the back seat. "I have an idea!" She encouraged the band to put their luggage in one pile and then she took out a few unicorn pearls and rubbed the bags with them. All their equipment lightly levitated off the ground, giving way to a gentle push.

"Great thinking!" Key said. "Now we can push our gear as if it were on carts."

"I had a feeling some unicorn magic would come in handy right about now," Candii said.

The band trekked through the asphalt desert all the way to the stadium as the morning sun began to rise behind it.

"How's everyone feeling?" Sir Taco asked.

"I'm feeling great!" Candii said.

Thad nodded. "I think naps are just what we needed!"

"I know I certainly feel better," Key said. "Although, I could really go for some breakfast. Do you think they sell ballpark hotdogs in here?"

"It's a stadium," Thad said. "They usually sell hot dogs, corn dogs, brat dogs, pickle dogs. You know, all kinds of dogs."

Sir Taco smacked his lips. "I could really go for a California dog! An all-beef frank topped with avocado and a fried egg!"

"I don't know if you'll find anything that fancy in here," Thad smiled. "We're probably talking guilty-pleasure park food, so don't get your hopes up."

After some exploration, they stumbled upon a crowd waiting in line to enter the stadium. The band took their place in line.

Sir Taco tapped the person ahead of him. "So, what exactly are we waiting in line for?"

"What kind of question is that? You mean to tell me you got in this line and don't even know what it's for?"

"For the sake of argument, let's just say yes."

"Okay. First off, that's weird. Second off, this is the line to get into the famous Metal Stadium where they record episodes of the greatest television show on the continent, Metal Chef."

"Thanks." Sir Taco turned around and huddled with the band. "So, Thad, you're saying the unicorn pearl is inside this stadium?"

"That's what I'm seeing," Thad confirmed after consulting his GPS once more.

"Well, apparently they're filming a tv show in there. That's a bit out of our element, wouldn't you say?"

"That's fine," Candii said. "We'll just head on in as members of the audience and take a moment to scope the place out. We don't even know yet where inside it is or who has it."

The band agreed and thus waited in a very long line for a very long time. They finally received their tickets sometime around noon and were ushered inside a massive dome filled with culinary wonders and delights on a center field. Scores of cooking prep stations and kitchen appliances sat in the center of the vertigo-inducing bleacher section.

"This reminds me of a soccer stadium but with tile instead of grass and cooks instead of soccer players," Thad said.

Key sighed. "Thank you for that incredibly obvious observation."

The band took their seats practically in the stratosphere and awaited the show.

An announcement came over the loudspeakers. "Welcome, culinary enthusiasts and aspiring chefs, to the live taping of Metal Chef, season eleven!" The crowd shook the stadium with cheers. "I'm proud to welcome the current champions of Stadium Kitchen, the undefeated Metal Chef Duo, Morty and Rashad!"

All the way down below, the band struggled to see a pair of small, white-clothed blips enter the stadium and wave to the crowd. The stadium once again erupted with pride and Candii worried that the building would not hold together if such a ruckus happened again.

"And today we are excited to announce a brand-new challenge mode that I know every single one of you in the crowd is going to love! I am pleased to reveal the Audience Glory or Eject Challenge where a member of the audience will be chosen to compete against our Metal Chefs on a specially designed stage! Their two kitchens are constructed on giant spring traps!" The roof of the stadium retracted and gave way to the cloudy sky above. "And what will happen to the loser? Well, take a look above! They'll be launched into the ocean far away from here! Enjoy the swim back to the continent!" The crowd could not contain themselves as they laughed with amazement.

"Sucky succulent. I think I'm going to be sick." Candii held her stomach and turned green as the bleachers continued to sway. She grabbed the bag Sir Taco's twelve hot dogs came in, but it was full of ketchup packets. She thrusted it back and desperately searched for a bucket as the turbulence intensified.

"And today's lucky challenger is inside this envelope. Let's see… Oh! There seems to have been a change in plans. One moment, please." The announcer covered the microphone. Mumbling and whispering came over the speakers. After a minute, the announcer returned. "How surprising, yet fitting! I'm told that a special request has been made that we literally can't refuse for fear of divine punishment! For the first time ever, a group of seats will take the stage in a team battle! Those seats are…"

Candii vomited into the bleachers as the spotlights turned on the band. Their faces were plastered on the jumbo screen.

17 Rigged Judgement from on High

"Are you sure you're going to be all right?" Sir Taco asked Candii as they put on their aprons and took an inventory of the cookware available on the show floor kitchen. "I have a weird feeling about this."

"I don't have a choice. The prize for winning the competition is the unicorn pearl. We either win this thing or risk it being given to someone else." Candii felt weak on her knees and took a moment to compose herself. "I'm fine. I'll be fine."

"Your condition does seem rather unusual. I've never known you to get motion sick," Thad said.

Candii waved them away. "I think I'm just exhausted from this trip, that's all. Let's just get cooking!"

The announcer stepped onto the stage and shook Sir Taco's hand. "Thank you for joining us on the stage of Stadium Kitchen today, folks. What was your team name again? Sorry, I forgot."

Sir Taco scratched his head. "We're the world-famous band, The Non-Traditional Key Gullz. You've really never heard of us?"

"I don't listen to music, sorry. So, any questions before we begin?"

Key pushed Sir Taco out of the way. "Just one. How do we win again?"

"You must cook a dish for our three mystery judges behind that veiled raised platform over there. During the competition, they will reveal clues regarding their hunger preferences for today. Whoever gets the most votes for their overall meal wins."

"So you're telling me we're cooking for three people and we don't even know what they like?"

"Are you sure you've never seen this show before? Like, everyone knows Metal Chef," the announcer scoffed.

Sir Taco pushed Key behind him. "You could say we're not from around here. I guess Metal Chef has a limited reach."

The announcer sneered at the jab. "If you'll excuse me." The announcer stepped off the kitchen spring trap and walked toward the crowd. "Are you ready?"

The crowd cheered.

"In three…two…one…go!"

The lights facing the crowd went dim and the band felt as if they and the culinary duo, Morty and Rashad, on a spring trap platform next to them, were the only people in the world.

Rashad walked his way over to the band. In a strangely gruff Jersey accent, he said, "Hey, folks. Thanks for being good sports and agreeing to come on down here. I'm sure you'll have a great time."

Right behind him, short Morty skipped on over and followed up with a fittingly high-pitched, manic voice. "Yeah! Enjoy the free flight and pool party! Yeah!"

"We have work to do, gentlemen. Now if you don't mind?" Thad shooed them away.

"So, what's on the menu?" Key asked with three chopsticks and a whisk in her hands.

Candii thought for a moment. "Until we get any clues, I say we play it safe and start preparing rice and broccoli as our sides."

Everyone agreed and they began boiling water and chopping vegetables. The band was well on their way when the announcer's voice came over the loudspeaker again.

"What's that on the big screens up above? Our first set of clues!" Icons appeared for fish, broccoli, chocolate, and a fig. "Can our chefs incorporate these suggestions from the judges to capture their votes?"

"This menu is stressing me out!" Key cried. "Does anyone mind if I set a little beat while I cook?"

"I think I can chop and whistle at the same time, too," Thad said.

"I've handled a pot and hummed. Let's do it!" Candii nodded.

"Leave the vocals to me," Sir Taco said. "Just don't expect me to taste test because my mouth will be busy!"

"Thanks!" Key smiled as she tapped her spoons on make-shift bowl drums. "Let's dedicate this one to the judges and whatever the heck they want."

Begin Any Way You Want It by Journey

INTRODUCTION & VERSE 1
Any ... things!

"Fish, broccoli, chocolate, and a fig?" Candii wondered. "Thad, weren't you a chef once?"

"That was a long time ago, Candii. I'm not sure if I still have it in me." Thad did some quick search engine research and wrote down a brief menu based on those ingredients. The band checked it out and it seemed reasonable. "I mean, this might work, but I don't know."

"This looks amazing! What do we need to do?" Candii asked.

PRE-CHORUS
Ooh ... tight!

Thad said, "There's still more clues to come, so we need to limit how much we rely on these items. Let's chocolate coat some figs. Then, deep fry the fish, chop it up, and mix it with the rice and broccoli."

"Killer plan!" Key smiled. "I'm getting hungry already!"

CHORUS
Any ... it!

The band grabbed handfuls of ingredients from the shared pantry.

Sir Taco chopped ginger and measured the spices.

Key cleaned a fish and dropped it in the fryer.

Thad made a chili sauce and sliced lemons.

Candii dipped the figs in chocolate and plated them.

"Fabuloso!" Candii admired.

VERSE 2
I ... things!

"Another set of clues!" the announcer interrupted. "What could they be?" The screens above displayed a pickle, orange juice, a strawberry, and chili pepper.

"Good," Thad nodded. "We already have the chili. Let's deep fry the pickle as well and mix an orange-strawberry lemonade."

PRE-CHORUS

Ooh ... tight!

The band was chopping away furiously, minding their own business, when chef Morty wandered over to their station from the shadows and swiped their salt without them noticing.

Candii heard the crowd laughing but she did not know why.

CHORUS

Any ... it!

"Pass me the salt, please," Key asked.

"Shoot, I can't find it anywhere!" Sir taco said, peeking under pots.

"We need that salt!" Thad said. "Keep looking!"

The band frantically overturned their stations but nobody could find the salt.

"What are we going to do?" Key asked.

INSTRUMENTAL

♫ ♫ ♫

"I'm so confused! I know it was just here!" Candii said.

She opened every cabinet and checked underneath every cooking utensil to no avail.

BRIDGE

She ... on!

Thad yelled suddenly, "Hold on! I got an idea!"

He took a napkin and jotted down a plan to extract salt from the pickles.

INSTRUMENTAL

♪ ♪ ♪

Using a magical process called reverse-osmosis-purifying-ul-traviolet-carbon-filtering-distilled-and-fermented-desalina-tion, a technique Thad had picked up during a brief stint as a short-order cook, they were able to extract pure salt from the pickles.

CHORUS x4

Oh ... it!

The announcer boomed one last time. "Just one ingredient this time? You know what that means! It's a Priority Ingredient that must be incorporated!"

The screens revealed black licorice!

"What? That is insane!" Thad said. "How are we supposed to incorporate such a strong flavor this late? It's sure to bleed into anything we combine it with."

Candii spied on the other chefs and saw they had already prepared a licorice themed dessert. A box of licorice and a handwritten note sat behind their station.

"Curse you, announcer!" Candii cried. She shook her fists into the sky. "This whole thing was rigged!"

Everyone turned to Thad who was sweating bullets. The pressure and the lights seemed brighter. He took a deep breath to calm himself. An idea filled his mind. "Give me a unicorn pearl!"

Candii reached into her pocket and handed him a unicorn pearl. He rubbed it on a rope of black licorice. He tried the candy and it was incredibly mild. "Use this as a lemonade straw!"

They cut up the rope and put a licorice straw in every strawberry-orange lemonade. A buzzer sounded. The competition was over. The band felt the platform underneath shudder. Their stomachs dropped. The spring trap apparatus was being prepared for possible use.

End Any Way You Want It by Journey

The announcer spoke over the loudspeaker. "My fair audience, it's time for the judging! Let me introduce our judges. Our first judge loves all things citrus and writes lyrics to express that love! Please welcome Orangello T. Money!" The far-left veil on the judge's stage lifted and revealed a rapper, who apparently was also a food connoisseur. He waved smoothly.

"Where there's food, there's fire. And that means we have to have everyone's favorite emergency responder, Fire Chief Shannon!" The center veil lifted and a smiling lady waved to the crowd.

"Lastly, there's no way we could tape an audience special without a very special guest who earned her place in the history books as the very first audience all-star." The crowd cheered in pandemonium. "That's right! I can tell you know who it is! I am proud to announce last season's winner of the Audience Tournament, Queen Morgana Malevolent!" The last veil lifted and Morgana stood, waving to the crowd and blowing a kiss to the band.

She waved her hand and floated a microphone to her. "Thank you very much. I'm happy to be back to uphold the integrity of all home cooks who dare challenge our magnificent Metal Chefs."

Candii gasped. "This is the most biased farce I've ever had the displeasure to be a part of!"

Studio stagehands carted the two side's food to the judge's table and served the meal by Metal Chefs Morty and Rashad first.

Orangello took the first bite. "Mmm. Dawg, the broccoli is perfectly tender. I always enjoy a light seasoning too."

Chief Shannon spooned a red dish. "I can tell you really turned up the heat with this main course. I'm all about heat so this dish has a thumbs up from me."

Morgana slipped a forkful of poultry into her mouth and slowly curled her smile. "Mmm, yes. This is simply divine. I couldn't possibly ask for anything more. Don't you agree, Orangello?"

"I do have to agree with you, dawg. This is the high-level cuisine we should expect from two Metal Chefs."

Morgana held her nose up. "Then, I propose we end this competition right now. There is no point in trying whatever those dubious blobs are on the other plates. Don't you agree?" She put her fork down on her plate and shot a wry glance at the band.

"Hold the fire, Morgana," Chief Shannon interrupted. "I didn't come here today to leave on a half-full stomach. I'm fully committed to trying both dishes."

"Yeah, me too, dawg."

The camera turned toward her and zoomed in. Morgana saw her face enlarged on the big screen. Her stomach audibly growled. Her smile melted away as she irritatingly resigned to their wishes. "Very well. I suppose I'm still a little peckish."

The stagehands then served the dishes created by the band.

First, they tried the chili-fish and broccoli main course with the fried pickle on the side.

"This is spicy!" Fire Chief Shannon cried. "Somebody call my station because I feel a red-hot love sparking for this dish!"

"I find the fish perfectly cooked and deboned. Nothing gets me more than a bone in my gums, you know what I'm saying, dawg?" Orangello asked.

Morgana tasted the fish and frowned. "No. I don't know what you're saying, *dawg*."

Next, they tried the chocolate covered figs.

"Dawg. Dawg!" Orangello looked at the fig in his hand, and then to each judge, and then back to the fig. "Dawg, I love figs. When I put it on the screen, I was expecting some type of wacky transformation that they typically do on this show, but these figs are left alone and enhanced with this slightly bitter chocolate! This really made my day!"

Morgana sneered. "Maybe to you, but I expect more creativity from my cooks."

Finally, they tried the lemonade. Morgana quickly took a sip through the licorice straw and coughed. "Wow! I'm overwhelmed by the bitterness of licorice! What an outrageous idea! This was not what I had in mind when I put black licorice on the screen."

Orangello shook his head. "You know, dawg, I can barely taste it."

"I have to agree with Orangello, Morgana. What slight bitterness I taste seems to really enhance the sweetness and tartness of the drink itself. This is a fine way to end a smoking hot entry into the competition today."

All the remaining food was carted away and the announcer deliberated with the judges quietly about their scores.

Finally, the announcer stepped off the judge's stage and walked toward the two kitchens. "Thank you for waiting, everyone! Our judges are ready to review today's competition! Are you excited?"

Sir Taco sweated profusely. "I don't want to blast off again." The band held hands and steadied themselves on the giant platform.

"Let's hear from each one and find out who they're voting for!"

Morgana went first. "I have to say, I am sorely disappointed in our guest home chefs. I really wish I had more praise to share, however they didn't really transform any of the ingredients to what I would consider Metal Chef quality. This show has long prided itself with the ability of a chef to take the mundane and turn it into the extraordinary and to show a brand-new world to the judges. Today I fear we have significantly lowered the bar and hope our contestants feel bad because they did bad."

The announcer was startled by the sheer savagery on display. She took a moment to compose herself before responding. "Wow. That is the most scathing review I have ever heard on the history of this show. I think it's clear where your vote goes. And may the guest chefs have mercy on their souls."

"Yes. I vote for the Metal Chefs, Morty and Rashad," Morgana said.

"Yeah! Thanks, Queen, yeah!" Chef Morty said.

"We'll see you for that catering gig next week!" Chef Rashad said delightfully. The chef duo took a bow.

The announcer pointed to the next judge. "Fire Chief Shannon, what is your vote?"

The Fire Chief glanced briefly at Morgana and then swallowed a huge glass of water. "I feel it necessary to address the point my esteemed colleague Morgana made regarding the duty of our contestants to transform ingredients and introduce new profiles to the judges. I too agree that this show has had a long and storied tradition of doing just that. However, today I struggled with the idea that the very tradition always trumps the cult of the new. We're in a new season, with new challenges, and a new Stadium

Kitchen set. I can't help but also feel the theme of *new* creeping into how we judge.

"I asked myself during the meal what it was that I was judging. Was it truly the use of food in clever or creative ways? I actually got on my phone and looked up this very show to read again what the purpose was. It says plainly on our website that the goal is to match the favorite flavors with the judges. Nowhere does it require a novel reinvention of the ingredients. I must admit that I very much enjoyed the direct approach by our home chefs. They gave us what we asked for in the simplest of terms. If I were at home and wanted a prepared meal after a long day, quite frankly I prefer the home chef's dish to our Metal Chefs, Morty and Rashad. I vote for The Non-Traditional Key Gullz."

The audience erupted in a mixture of gasps and jeering.

Morgana smirked and shrugged her shoulders playfully. "I guess we can't win them all," she giggled. "Let's get this over with."

"Thank you, Fire Chief Shannon," the announcer continued. "Orangello, no pressure, but please share with us your tie-breaking choice."

"Oh, Orangello," Morgana said. "I have a meeting with the Rockin' Records board tomorrow about some top-level topics and I think it would just be a grand opportunity to share my opinion of you and your work with them. I hope that's okay."

"Oh, um…sure, dawg. I'd appreciate that." Orangello shifted uncomfortably in his chair when he leaned forward to grip his micro-phone. Speaking softly, he said, "I was pretty undecided going into the post-meal phase because I found both delights and detriments to both team's dishes. It wasn't until I heard my fellow judges' commentary that I was able to clarify my position on the matter. I think we've already talked enough so I'm just gonna come out and say I vote for the home chefs."

Stadium Kitchen exploded with cheers and jeers as a very rare outcome occurred. The announcer declared The Non-Traditional Key Gullz as the winners and, by the press of a lever, Morty and Rashad were skyrocketed up and out of the stadium somewhere to a waiting rescue boat far out in the open ocean water.

"We did it!" Candii shouted.

"Great coaching, Thad!" Sir Taco said with a hug.

"I couldn't have done it without the inspiration of great music. My thanks goes to Key for getting our groove on."

"It was nothing, just my natural instinct," she replied.

The announcer presented the band with the unicorn pearl as Morgana wrapped herself in her cloak and evaporated in a burst of flames. The judge's stage caught on fire and the stadium's fire suppression system began alarming and sprinkling everyone with water. The audience fled the bleachers toward their nearest emergency exit.

With droplets running down her face, Candii held the glowing pearl and felt a unicorn's presence inside. "This one's for Elegant."

The band exited the stadium and walked back to the van.

"We now have fourteen unicorn pearls," Thad counted. "We should be tied with Morgana, save the one at the base of her mountain. I don't know what it's doing there and not in her lair, but that gives us the opportunity to grab it and one-up her in the final confrontation."

Candii fist pumped in the air. "Let's hit the road!"

18 Castle in the Sky with Pearls

The band drove all through the afternoon and into the late evening. They returned south to the base of the menacing Mount Rock. The looming volcano spewed lava bits into space. Deadly meteorites rained down like shrapnel along the solitary road leading to the castle just beneath the summit. Bats swirled among the black towers jutting out from the center stone palace. The night's bright, full moon mixed its eerie white brilliance with the red glow of molten lava brewing just out of sight.

The band dug through the van and took stock of their instruments. Confident with their supplies knowing this was their last chance to turn around until the job was done, they gazed upon the intimidating sight before them.

"That is one heck of a back porch," Key said looking toward the summit.

"Once we find the last free unicorn pearl somewhere in our present general area," Thad said, "we'll need to take our ascent slow to watch out for those lava meteors.

Sir Taco shuddered. "One hit and the van will be a burnt pancake."

"Never mind that. Where exactly is the pearl?" Candii asked.

Thad checked his GPS. "It's not far. Actually, see that boulder over there? It might just be right behind it."

"Could it be buried in the dirt?" Key asked.

"Maybe it shot right down and burrowed into the cliffside," Sir Taco suggested.

A large, dusty boulder sat in the middle of the road. As the band approached it, a frightening roar shook their souls.

Candii stumbled to the ground.

The roar bellowed again even louder. They covered their ears.

"What is that?" Candii screamed.

From behind the boulder, a large ogre emerged brandishing an oversized guitar in the shape of a medieval battle axe. Ingrained in the fretboard was the unicorn pearl. The ogre, like the pearl, glowed eerily. Rainbow wisps flowed from the pearl down the strings, across his hands, and covered him like an aura.

The ogre pointed at the band. "You're The Non-Traditional Key Gullz!"

Candii rose to her feet and gripped her guitar. "That's right! What's it to you?"

"You're here to disrupt the Queen's plans!"

"Wow. Nothing gets past you."

"I won't let you! I will protect the Queen!" He gripped his mighty axe and strummed a single chord. Funhouse mirror-like soundwaves penetrated the band. Their bones rattled and their teeth chattered. Dirt and pebbles blew past them as they braced themselves, barely able to stay standing.

Candii and the band gripped their instruments and turned the amp volume so high they cracked the knobs. They were about to show this poor soul the power of rocking at level eleven!

"This is it, band!" Candii rallied. "This is the last obstacle before Morgana herself! Are you with me?"

"No!" the ogre bellowed. "The Queen deserves her peace!"

19 I'm Wide Awake

At age seven, Morgana Benevolent was the spitting image of her father whom she had never known. Her mother saw that man in her daughter's face every day, and that was the only thing that kept the spark of life inside her aflame.

Godric the Kind died during the Rock War of End Times tending to the wounds of the enemy in a trench. During a retreat, he was unable to keep up with his battalion, and so he hid in a trench waiting for a more opportune time to flee again. To his surprise, a wounded soldier too injured to attack crawled toward him. Godric's strong belief in his Hippocratic Oath prohibited him from turning a blind eye to the dying woman, and so he tried to patch her up. Upon further inspection, her wounds were so severe that his efforts were in vain.

Perhaps because of this delay, he missed his chance to flee. An enemy platoon descended upon him and ended his life in the trench fearing he had killed the very soldier he had tried to save.

Word of her husband's death destroyed his wife, Nina Benevolent, and left her magically sterile. The source of her magic, as was the tradition with the Benevolent family line, was from the concentration of intense emotion in her heart. It was not enough to simply feel strongly, but one must also have control to channel just one emotion at a time. Intense, cycling emotions of sadness, grief, anger, loss, confusion, and more prevented her from ever feeling just one way for very long. Once a revered magical lawyer, the constant emotional turmoil within her prevented her from scrying the pasts of her clients to help them argue innocence, and so she resigned from law and fell into a deep depression.

In an attempt to spare her daughter from a similar endless cycle of sadness and futility, she moved them out of the city and into the countryside where she could surround them both with nature's beauty and innocence. Unfortunately, it was not the environment that she needed to flee, but the feelings inside her heart. Nina's coping mechanisms followed her and she heavily abused magical memory-dulling substances to just barely operate day to day.

After her mind reached its inevitable limit, she laid on her bed and called young Morgana to her side. She turned to her daughter and impressed upon her the view of the world as she saw it.

Begin The A-Team by Ed Sheeran

INSTRUMENTAL

♬ ♬ ♬

"Morgana, my beautiful daughter."

"Yes, mama?"

"This world is not fair. I know I've always told you different, but now I know that we are not owed anything and you must fight for your right to live."

VERSE 1

White ... men.

With the last of her strength she took her daughter's hand.

"You must go to magic college. Learn to use your gift. I'm sorry I won't be there to guide you. Look for the joy in your heart and focus in on it. Never embrace fear, never let it take you over. You can't. We can't."

"Yes, mama."

Nina Benevolent passed away leaving behind her daughter alone in their country home. In the days to come, Nina's substance suppliers would come to her home looking for her. They found only Morgana.

PRE-CHORUS

And ... us.

Morgana lived a life of servitude and mistreatment at the hands of the same people who hastened her mother's death. After a day of constant labor on the streets, at night she would look at the starry sky and imagine a place where she could find the joy her mother spoke of.

She wallowed in a sea of sadness, fear, and resentment for her captors. Over time, specific feelings would boil over and crowd the others out. When this happened, somewhere deep inside her soul she would feel a warming that she could not explain. It caused a tingling sensation to her fingertips and toes.

CHORUS

Cause ... fly.

Was this the magic her mother spoke of? In passing, she would ask her captors questions about wonderful professions that used magic she would read about on street flyers. None of them had ever practiced magic before so they did not have anything to say.

With each year, she began to practice channeling her resentment into small tricks. She would make objects go invisible in plain sight, burn the stove extra hot and evaporate the soup, or sometimes conjure sounds of beasts in the middle of the night to frighten her captors. Even with these tricks, she was fearful of being discovered as their source.

VERSE 2

Ripped ... phone.

At age ten, Morgana was ordered to clean a filthy rec room. She opened the door and saw discarded magical substance containers strewn carelessly about the floor. As she always did when told to handle these bottles of evil that took her mother, she cried and pleaded not to be sent into the room, but her captors tossed her inside.

She picked herself up off the floor and angrily kicked the bottles away. Suddenly, a sickness in her stomach boiled to the surface and she coughed a searing fireball onto a pool table. As the flames engulfed the room and then into the house proper, she heard the screams of her captors. She stood engulfed in the flames, unaffected and protected by her feeling of joy in hearing their cries of agony.

PRE-CHORUS

And ... us.

Was this the joy that her mother spoke of?

Morgana walked out of her prison, the building ablaze and spreading to the neighborhood around her, with a smile on her face from cheek to cheek. Surely this was the joy her mother told her to find, for her mind was filled with a wonderful feeling of liberation and discovery, silencing her heart still drowning in pain.

CHORUS

Cause ... fly.

Morgana decided to explore as she closed her eyes and imagined herself soaring higher and higher. She felt herself being lifted off the ground, filled with a fire in her lungs.

Opening her eyes in a fright, the city's horizon grew larger below her as she truly began to float above it all. She observed the few city blocks that had become her world the past three years aflame.

Between fits of laughter, she felt the burning in her lungs grow unbearably uncomfortable. She let out a roar of defiance over the city and balls of fire spewed across the buildings that she resented so.

BRIDGE & INSTRUMENTAL

An ... ♫ ♫ ♫

Her body seethed with magic pouring from her fingertips like water. It rolled out of her eyes and mouth like steam.

She saw her dreams from the last three years coming true right before her eyes and by her own hands. The satisfaction was intoxicating.

Law enforcement from all over the land descended onto the city. A few caught a glimpse of her terrifying face, but none were able to get close enough to capture her or, at the very least, learn her true identity.

PRE-CHORUS

And ... us.

Once she was satisfied, Morgana flew far away into the deep uninhabited Rhythm Forest of the neighboring Death province.

Alone, dirty, and uncared for, she spent four years refining her resentful heart against the wild beasts of death metal.

She was never taught to play a musical instrument or how to develop a rhythm and thus she was rejected by all the creatures of the forest big and small.

Thankfully, with enough time, she found that the ambient sounds of the forest provided a deep beat to which she eventually developed a musical prowess in order to survive.

CHORUS & CODA

And ... die.

At fifteen, Morgana met an ogre that she finally could not best.

As he raised his axe guitar to rid the forest of the devil, she threw up her small hands in deference.

The ogre saw fear in her eyes that he knew all too well. Instead of striking her, he extended his hand.

She grasped tightly and felt something in her heart she had not known since she was a girl.

Reacquainting herself with kindness and disrupting the singular burning passion of resentment in her heart, she decided to return to the world of people and complete her mother's dying wish to attend magic high school and then college.

After years of isolation, no one recognized the young woman with no background. She was able to enroll in high school and succeed all the way to the Boston College of Magic, the continent's premier school.

End The A-Team by Ed Sheeran

20 Hard Rock Falling from the Sky

Come at me, you accursed foreigners!" the ogre bellowed.

"Actually, we identify more with Journey, but it doesn't really matter!" Sir Taco retorted.

Key tapped her drumsticks three times.

Begin Famous Last Words by My Chemical Romance

Introduction & Verse 1

Now ... speak!

The ogre roared and let out a massive strum of his battle axe guitar. The band shuddered and shielded their faces from the terrifying reverberation.

Feeling a tremendous gush of air, Candii removed her hand from her face. The ogre descended from the sky with the axe swinging high over his head.

"Move!" she cried.

The band picked up their instruments and dispersed before the ogre split the pavement between them. He quickly dislodged his axe and swung it in a wide arc. The blade barely missed Sir Taco's head.

"Shooty McShoot face!" Sir Taco screamed as he checked his head for missing hair.

"We need the high ground to win!" Thad pointed to the road above.

Candii ran to the van and took out her backpack full of unicorn pearls. She strapped the bag on and followed the band as they hustled around the ogre and up the winding road.

Once safely above the monster, the band threw their amps down onto the dirt and jammed. The cliffside below trembled sending a rockslide into the ogre's face.

The ogre swung his axe and smashed the boulders overhead. "Nothing will stop me from protecting the downtrodden!"

The ogre threw his axe up at the band like a tomahawk. Key was blown back when the axe smashed her drums into a million pieces. The ogre threw himself up against the cliffside and clawed up furiously.

Thad helped Key to her feet. "What are we going to do?" he asked. "We're down a drummer!"

CHORUS

I ... home!

Sir Taco dug in his pocket and pulled out two spoons he had stolen from Stadium Kitchen for the laughs.

"Can you make these work?" he asked Key.

"There's nothing I can't drum!" Key took the spoons and jammed on any surface available to keep the bands beat.

The ogre pulled himself onto the ledge and picked up his axe.

Sir Taco took the lead and stepped defiantly in front of the beast. The band jammed in harmony and the ogre covered his ears unable to take the volume at such a close range. His axe slipped from his hands and he tripped backwards down the cliff. The hulk landed on the tour van, smashing it into a flapjack.

VERSE 2

Can ... weak!

"We're just going to have to rush our way to the top on foot!" Candii commanded while picking up her amp and hoofing it.

The band scurried up the mountainside higher and higher turning to check on the ogre who was coming to his senses.

Once he regained his balance, he glared at the band and reacquainted himself with his weapon. He knelt and then leapt high onto the mountainside. Hopping after them like a tree frog, he ascended quickly.

Despite the band trying to be quick, an explosion erupted above. Flaming lava boulders were hurtling through the air. A huge molten rock landed right in front of them stopping them in their tracks.

Candii turned around to see the ogre rushing them. "Stand your ground!" she demanded.

The band leaned into their instruments and did the only thing they could do: jam.

CHORUS x2

I ... home!

The intense passion slowed the ogre to a crawl but he kept his head down and stepped toward the band with his axe in hand, one steady foot at a time.

Thad's fingers blazed the strings upon his guitar, but a string turned red and popped off. "W-we're in trouble now!"

Sir Taco raised his voice, but he felt a crackle. His throat had run dry due to the searing volcanic air.

The band took risky steps back toward the molten boulder to give them any space from the ogre. With no other options, the band huddled close hoping to increase their musical potency.

INSTRUMENTAL

♫ ♫ ♫

Only a few steps away, the ogre steadied himself upright. His eyes barely open, every muscle off his body rippled from the pure rock power of the band. He slowly raised his axe above his head and took aim at Candii who, filled to the brim with both fear and boldness, stepped forward and jammed harder to protect the band.

"Get behind me! Step back as far as you can...!" She turned around. They could not step back into the lava ball any farther.

BRIDGE

These ... me.

Candii closed her eyes and whispered a wish from deep within her.

"Unicorns. Lend me your innocent hearts. Be one with mine and trust in me."

The ogres axe plummeted toward Candii's head. Yet, it failed to reach her. Her senses felt as if time was slowed to a halt.

She felt the warmth of the unicorn pearls on her back. Magic radiated from her bag and, one by one, the unicorn pearls flew out and hovered above the band.

BRIDGE 2 x4

I... dead!

Key looked up in awe as the pearls shone brighter than she had ever seen. Her spoons popped out of her hands and were replaced with drumsticks made of diamond. Magically before her appeared a new celestial drum set. Each corner of the instrument was drawn from a star in the night sky plummeting down and taking its place for the greater good.

The strings of Thad's guitar melted off in the heat. Wiry white unicorn hairs split out of the bridge and crawled up the fretboard. They twisted themselves into knots within the tuning pegs.

A bottle of refreshing unicorn milk appeared in Sir Taco's hand. He chugged the whole bottle in a second and smacked his lips.

As if time was a popping bubble, the ogre's axe plummeted again toward Candii, who threw her arms up as her final defense.

A blinding flash of rainbow and glitter, the axe collided with a barrier of unicorn magic. In that fleeting moment, Candii's heart connected to the ogre's through their two powers. She felt hope and compassion, but pity most intensely of all. For whom such worry was for, she was unable to determine.

The axe deflected off the barrier and the blade carved a deep gash in the ground beside Candii. Caught off balance, the ogre stumbled slightly.

Candii turned to the band and they nodded back. They twisted their amp's volume knobs until they popped off. Waves of rhythmic rock roared from their instruments.

The ogre stumbled again as one of his hands lost the grip of his axe. He struggled to hold on with his remaining hand until he was hit again with a stylish rhythmic blast and his arms flew back over his head.

CHORUS

I ... home!

His knees began to buckle and his body lost balance. The ogre fell onto his side into the dirt and tumbled down the road as if in a wild rapid.

Candii took one firm step forward and sent a massive reverb rumbling down the path. The ogre tumbled farther toward the cliffside. She took another brave step and reverbed the ogre over the edge.

A flash of emotions pumped through her body like a heartbeat. A memory of her fleeting connection with the ogre overwhelmed her and she tossed her guitar aside. She ran down the road to the cliff's ledge. As she approached, the ogre's hand jutted up and grasped the ledge desperately.

"I felt your feelings!" Candii shouted over the deafening music. "Who are you?"

"You'll take everything from her! She'll have nothing left to live for!" the ogre cried, barely audible.

"What are you talking about? I don't understand!"

"Her heart!" The last blast of music from behind Candii blew the ogre's hand from the edge and he fell seemingly endlessly to what Candii surmised was the last drop of his final album.

End Famous Last Words by My Chemical Romance

Candii collapsed on the ground near the cliff edge and the band rushed to her side.

"Candii! Are you okay?" Sir Taco asked. He placed a hand on her back.

"I...I think I am. I'm just so tired," Candii said with her head in her hands.

"You must have expelled a lot of empathy to get the unicorn pearls to do those awesome tricks," Thad said pointing to the pearls that had returned to their dimmed state scattered along the road. "I imagine that you're drained for the moment,"

"You're probably right." Candii slowly rose to her feet. "Let's take this slow so I can regain some strength."

The band walked back to the ogre's abandoned guitar and pried the pearl from its fretboard.

Candii held it in her palm and said, "This one is for Lovely." She stowed it away in her backpack along with all the others. She turned to the band. "We now have fifteen unicorn pearls. Since we're unable to detect the last one anywhere on the continent, that means Morgana only has fourteen."

She stood tall and commanded at the top of her lungs, her fist flying through the air, "With our instruments and these pearls, we will surely blast her back to the stone age of rock!"

21 It's All on the Table…Eventually

She band ascended the mountain road cautiously. Thankfully, there were no more surprises except the errant lava meteor, but those were easy enough to spot from above.

When they finally reached the top, they approached a black granite castle with high pointy peaks and tall foreboding double-doors. Sir Taco used the door knocker just for kicks, but no one answered. It took all four of them shoving together to get the doors moving. With one last heave, the doors swung back and they all fell on their behinds.

Key lifted her head and nervously surveyed the entryway. "It's dark in there."

"Who's first?" Sir Taco asked, jumping up and dusting off his pants.

Candii unpacked four unicorn pearls and gave each person one. "Follow me. She can't scare me."

The soft glow led the way forward as they slowly walked behind Candii. Deep into the lobby, Candii admired massive floor-to-ceiling paintings of various locations in the Land of Rock. "There's Jammertown and Candy Mountain," she pointed out.

"Oh, and a desert? Maybe that's what the frozen tundra igloos used to look like!" Key remarked about a particularly cheery looking one. Little elves with red noses held hands around an oasis.

Thad spotted a painting of New Rock City. Sir Taco admired a long canvas adorned with the green fields of The Pantry. They came across huge suits of armor that they feared could come to life at any moment.

Admittedly a bit lost, they walked into a warm room with a raging flame inside a massive stone fireplace. The walls were covered in books and flowing tapestries. Candii stepped near one and placed a tender hand on it. The artistry was unbelievable. It illustrated a story of magic, fire, and love that she could not quite put together.

Key stood at her side. "I think they're telling a sad story. One of love lost."

Candii let her eyes wander up to the top. A depiction of Morgana floating high above a flaming city was rendered impressively. "Well, it would make sense given the last words of the ogre. But none of that matters. We're here to right a massive wrong no, matter the circumstances."

Finding nothing helpful in that room, the band climbed a winding staircase into even greater darkness. And then music began to reach their ears. It sounded like a thunderous wind instrument.

"Is...is that an organ?" Candii asked bewildered.

"Ooo! Very villainesque!" Key chuckled.

"Hurry! This way!" Candii led the band quickly up another staircase as she followed the sound. The ominous composition grew louder as they passed through third, fourth, and fifth floor corridors. They briefly exited the castle and traveled over the ramparts overlooking the grounds. The sun had nearly set and the long shadows cast over the land were menacing.

"We have to end this before dawn. I don't think my unicorns have much time left. If we're too late..."

"They'll stay horses forever, won't they?" Sir Taco asked.

"That's right." Candii had no idea what she was going to have to do once she confronted Morgana, but she was willing to do anything to bring this struggle to an end.

Finally near the castle's peak, the band faced two massive wooden doors. On the other side, someone keyed the organ.

Candii turned to the band. "Are we ready? This is your last chance to head home. I've already asked you all to put yourselves in so much danger. Surely our greatest threat lies beyond this gate. I can't force any of you to step into the fire with me, but I do ask for your help."

Key smiled. She placed a hand on Candii's shoulder. "We'd never turn back now. We traveled every step of this journey at your side to see it to the end."

Sir Taco and Thad nodded.

They each gripped their instruments with their chapped, sore hands.

"Okay! Here we go!" Candii kicked in the door and the band rushed into a regally adorned chapel-like room with a breath-taking candle chandelier impossibly high above. A beautiful blood-red carpet ran through the room and intricate tapestries hung from the ceiling and adorned the walls. A tall figure, shrouded in a cloak and playing the organ, sat at the other end of the room. The figure was facing away from them.

"She's good," Sir Taco admitted.

"Yeah, maybe. She's alone, so I'm not too worried." Candii slowly approached the organ and stood only a few steps away from it. The figure abruptly stopped playing.

"Morgana!" she shouted. "We're here to end your game! We have fifteen unicorn pearls to your fourteen. Give them up and I'll go home. Resist and I'll be forced to rock your body!"

Morgana's cackle echoed through the room. She sounded like she was above, behind, and below them. She was everywhere at once.

"Where is that coming from?" Thad asked.

"Fools! You thought you could surprise me in my own lair? No, it is I who will demand the unicorn pearls from *you*! My fourteen are not enough for my plan. I need them all!"

"Enough!" Candii jumped forward and ripped the cloak away. She was surprised to see not Morgana but two gremlins, one standing on the other's shoulders. They snarled, snapping their drooling jaws, and hopped down to Candii's feet. They pranced around her tauntingly. Their quick movements startled her. She was unable to fight them off when they wrested her backpack away from her and sprinted across the room.

Sir Taco and Key gave chase and tackled the gremlins. After a beating, they retrieved the backpack and handed it back to Candii.

"Nice try, Morgana," Candii shouted toward the ceiling. "Now, are you going to face me like you did at the ranch?"

"Very well. I suppose every great leader has to step into the trenches and slay her own problems once in a while."

A bright flash of brilliance filled the room. The band shielded their eyes. Down from the ceiling descended Morgana in a shimmering light. She was surrounded by fourteen unicorn pearls swirling around her like an orbit. She gently planted herself on the ground between the band and the room's entrance.

"This is what you wanted, isn't it? A showdown of rock prowess? I suppose someone with as pitiful ambitions as your own, to keep a stale unicorn ranch selfishly to herself, would never be able to imagine what great miracles one could achieve with all that magical power."

Morgana raised her arm and flicked her fingers about. The pearls floated above her. They began to swirl in a circle and accelerated ever faster. She lifted off the ground and glided up.

"I truly did wish you would have stayed home and just moved on with your life, but I guess yours will just be another one I ruin. I wonder, when this is all over, if I'll finally be happy."

Candii gripped her bass, felt her heart skip a beat, and leaned forward. "Come at me!"

Begin Holding Out for a Hero by Bonnie Tyler

INSTRUMENTAL

♫ ♫ ♫

"Ha, ha, ha!" Morgana cackled as she darted to and fro among the rafters. She channeled the unicorn pearls and divined a celestial xylophone at her side. Scores of minions emerged from the shadows above, from the sides, and even, defying logic, from below the carpet with a collection of amps of all sizes.

They plugged in her xylophone with bundles of extension cords and the amps glowed with life from the overwhelming power of the unicorn pearls. The minions assembled in rows behind Morgana and formed a supporting chorus with voices that would not be prized for their clarity but certainly feared for their volume.

VERSE 1

Where … need.

The band jammed right back spewing hard rock out of their instruments way past their volume safety threshold! The sound was rattling their bones and brought back a hint of nostalgia from their rocking days long ago.

But were they too loud? Were their seasoned bones able to keep it together under the reverberations of this dangerous stunt?

Key's pummeling beat led the band steadily with her diamond drumsticks.

Sir Taco sang the words more clearly than he ever needed to before.

Thad felt the unicorn hair strings of his guitar smoothly assist with his transitions.

Candii opened her backpack and poured the unicorn pearls out at their feet. The pearls began to glow and give power to their instruments. She turned to the band and grinned.

"That's it! I can feel the power of the beat!"

CHORUS

I ... life!

Morgana's robes and hair rippled violently in recognition of their amazing performance.

"Not bad, Non-Traditional Key Gullz. But how about this?"

Morgana didn't even handle her mallets. They magically came to life in front of her, pounding on the xylophone with impossible speed. Their rhythm and precision were beyond anything the band had ever seen. All at once, her xylophone played the parts of an entire orchestra while being accompanied by a vast choir of echoing evil minions.

The band's feet slid several feet back pushed by the sheer awesome force pouring from Morgana's concert. They struggled to stay standing. Sir Taco was leaning forward almost forty-five degrees.

"That's not all. Why hold back when I'm having such fun!" she laughed with a maniacal grin. Morgana's unicorn pearls dispersed and flew erratically around the room.

The band tried to keep their eyes on the streaks of light, but the pearls were too fast to follow. On occasion, one would dart down and hit the band.

"Ow!" Candii cried as she was pelted by a series of pearls. Her fingers slipped and several notes were missing their marks.

VERSE 2

Somewhere … feet!

Candii threw her bass over her shoulder. She knelt and arranged her unicorn pearls in a circle. She stood in the center and wished with her whole heart for a miracle.

"Unicorns! Hear my wish! Lend me your strength!" The pearls began to glow and give speed to the band's hands. But a fury of Morgana's own pearls pelted the band and broke their concentration again.

"Ha, ha, ha!" Morgana cackled.

Candii tried to wish again but exhaustion began to overtake her. She was failing to muster enough concentrated empathetic energy to connect with her team back home.

She fell to her knees. Her head hung low. Her arms quivered.

"Oh no, oh no, oh no!" Sir Taco said. "We got a situation!"

CHORUS

I … night!

"Get her up!" Key demanded, her foot pounding on the step pedal like thunder.

Sir Taco ran to Candii's side and lifted her carefully up.

Morgana's pearls returned to her side. They pulsated and throbbed. Her volume output rose to impractical levels.

Sir Taco cupped his ears and let Candii fall to the hands and knees.

"What do we do now?" Thad frantically shouted. His fingers were slipping with increasing frequency.

"Minions!" Morgana commanded. "Now is the moment! Attack!"

Gremlins stormed the band. They hopped and leapt from every direction, encircling the group.

Sir Taco tried to push them away but he was quickly trampled. Thad swung his guitar and knocked a few minions back. More overwhelmed him and ripped his instrument from his hands.

They approached Key, sweat springing from her brow, but they could not have predicted her fury.

INSTRUMENTAL

♫ ♫ ♫

Key threw her head back and pounded her drumsticks upon the stars themselves. Twinkling, glittery shockwaves blew hordes of minions back. They collided into pillars and walls, eyes flung back and unconscious. Try as they might, the mob was unable to approach her.

Candii lifted her head upon the sight. Her vision was blurred but she felt hope building in her heart. "That's it! Just a little bit longer and I'll...I'm getting up!"

Morgana's face became twisted. "Who do you think you are? This is between Candii and I!" She summoned a minion and commanded, "Bring me the final unicorn pearl!"

"What?" Candii cried in shock.

BRIDGE

Up … blood!

The minion retrieved a black box for Morgana engraved with magical symbols. She revealed inside the final pearl belonging to the most powerful unicorn, Sparkles.

"You fools! I sealed away my trump card in magic-concealing runes to draw you into my trap! You never had the power to defeat me!"

The unicorn pearl flew up above her and she channeled its amazing power into her xylophone. All at once, Key's celestial instruments vanished into thin air.

With a broad wave of Morgana's arm, Key, Sir Taco, and Thad were lifted into the air and thrown back into the steel organ. They tumbled onto the floor. They tried to lift themselves but were completely defeated.

CHORUS x2

I … night!

"No!" Candii cried.

She stumbled to her feet and reached for her bass, but it too was missing. Her fourteen unicorn pearls were positioned around her but their glow started to wane until they finally grew dim and faded to gray. She lurched forward and stumbled over the pearls and onto her knee in the chaos.

She stretched her arm out toward Sparkle's unicorn pearl floating high above in the center of the enemy pearl orbit.

"Sparkles! Don't give your power to her!" she pleaded.

The unicorn pearl became clear and the face of Sparkles the unicorn appeared. Sparkles neighed sadly, helplessly, and the pearl became clouded again.

Candii stared desperately at Morgana. She felt totally powerless. "Please! No! You're torturing them! They don't want to be with you!"

Morgana cast a piercing gaze at Candii. "They don't know what they want." She reached up for the cathedral's ceiling. "Goodbye, Candii of The Non-Traditional Key Gullz. Give my regards to the afterlife."

She squeezed her hand into a fist and all thirty pearls in the room shone to life. Candii's fourteen flew past her, soared up above, and together all thirty swarmed into a massive ball. With a point of Morgana's finger, they violently zoomed like an arrow toward Candii.

Candii closed her eyes as the pearls pierced her heart.

"RIP," said one goblin.

"No!" the band cried.

End Holding Out for a Hero by Bonnie Tyler

22 Hello Mr. Sunshine

At first, there was only darkness. Then there was only light. Candii stumbled toward the light.

Could this be heaven? Is this what happens when you die? She shielded her eyes and walked into the blinding brightness but was then overcome with heat. She realized she was not in heaven, but somewhere else. She opened her eyes and was surprised to see burning brimstone, oceans of lava, and demons flying about.

"Holy heck in a hamper! What the heck happened to me?"

"That's a new swear," said a raspy, monotone voice from behind her.

Candii twirled and was startled by a tall demon with a clipboard, thick black glasses, and a tie, but no other clothes.

"Where am I?" she asked. "And who are you?"

The demon stretched out his open palm. Candii shook it.

"Hello. My name is Belthequazal-unarmobius, but you can call me Bell. I'm the Regional Intake Manager here in the lowest circle of the afterlife."

"I'm dead?" Candii asked with her hands running through her hair.

"Yes. Let's see…" Bell flipped through his clipboard. "Ah, here it is. You died in a rock band battle using unicorn magic." He raised his eyes to look at Candii. "Very dangerous," he whispered with disapproval. He scanned his clipboard again. "Um, you lived a good enough life that you were sent here to the ninth circle of the afterlife."

"Am I in the bad place?" Candii asked. She sat down on the floor, overwhelmed with feelings. She just held her head in her hands.

"Hell? Like the eternal place of torture and damnation? Ha, ha! No. I don't know if that exists, but I'm glad to say you are not there."

"Is this some type of Dante's Inferno?"

"Dante's Inferno…?" Bell thought about it for a moment. "Oh, you must be referring to the literary existence of the nine layers of hell. No, this isn't that either."

"Then what is this place?" Candii asked exasperated.

Bell cleared his throat. "Ahem. You now reside eternally in the ninth layer of the afterlife. All citizens, or tourists, in the Continent of the Jam Gods, if deceased, shall be resurrected in our care to live rocking righteous lives. At least, if they're evaluated to do so. The decor you see around you is merely the front of the house. I assure you, your quarters will be much more pleasing. Any resemblances to devils, hell, or other religious damnation locations are merely coincidental. We are just a system created to handle souls in the afterlife and we do not morally swing one way or the other."

"So, you're telling me this isn't a bad place to be?"

"Um…well, not entirely. Depending on a person's evaluation when they arrive, this may become a very uncomfortable afterlife for them indeed. We serve all kinds of souls and are equipped to reward or punish a wide variety of patrons. Okay. With that out of the way, I am now ready to give you your official evaluation."

She raised her head.

Bell reviewed his clipboard again. "Ms. Candii...no last name given. That's odd. Anyway, Ms. Candii, formerly of The Non-Traditional Key Gullz, I am pleased to announce your evaluation places you in the best level of the afterlife with all the fantastic benefits and rocking good times that..."

"Wait!" Candii interrupted. "What about The Non-Traditional Key Gullz? My bandmates! I left them up there..." She tried hard to recall her past. "...with...with Morgana! Did she send them here too?"

Bell flipped through his papers several times. "I don't see anything here about your friends. It appears they are still alive for the moment."

"Then they're still fighting her! They're in danger! I need to go back and help them!" Candii jumped to her feet and started running in circles while waving her arms, trying to find the light portal she stepped through.

Bell laughed. "Hold your horses! You can't go back. That's not how this works! You're dead now. This is where you stay."

Bell stared at Candii as her face contorted into sadness again. She collapsed on the ground and curled up into a ball.

"Oh, don't do that. You're gonna love it here!"

Candii sobbed uncontrollably as she rocked back and forth. Bell could not stand looking at her like this.

"Come on, kiddo. Cheer up, okay? Listen." Bell knelt down and pulled Candii up into a sitting position. "I can't send you back, but I can get you a room where you can view your friends for a little bit, if that'll help your transition. We're not supposed to show this to the customers, but I've heard your music before and I think it's pretty rockin'. Consider this a favor from a fan."

Bell helped Candii up and led her through a new portal of light and into an unremarkable, white, generic office lobby. All kinds of religious after life creatures walked the halls. There were angels, prophets, flying spaghetti monsters, and aliens, to name a few. They all had little ties and clipboards and many were leading around other people who were probably recently deceased.

"Please follow me, Candii. And try not to say anything or stare. Make it look like you know what you're doing because, you know, you're not supposed to be allowed where we're going."

Candii followed Bell through a series of doors and hallways until they opened a single door to a small white room with nothing but four white walls, a white chair, a large monitor, and a control panel. Bell gestured for Candii to sit down in front of it, which she did, and he pressed a series of buttons and twiddled knobs until the screen came to life.

On the screen, Candii saw images from all over the Continent of the Jam Gods. There were locations and landmarks from other provinces she had never visited. Bell focused the screen on Morgana's lair where Candii observed what remained of the band crumpled beneath Morgana's organ.

"Oh my gosh! Sir Taco, Thad, and Key! They're hurt!"

On screen, Morgana approached the trio and cackled.

"Well, Non-Traditional Key Gullz. Or should I call you the Traditional Key Gullz now? Wait...no, that doesn't sound right. Um, would it be the Untraditional Non-Traditional Key Gullz? How are you supposed to make it sound strange when you're already..." She spat and snarled. "Oh, never mind! I'll give you this, Candii, wherever you are: you and your little friends are cleverer than me when it comes to naming things but you still lack vision.

Gods! It must have been a nightmare for your public relations team to fit your long, stupid name on merch! What were you thinking?"

Sir Taco attempted to rise to his feet but he slumped back down. "That's why we go by the acronym NTKG, you dumb butt." He coughed and gripped his chest. "We won't let you abuse the unicorn pearls. In Candii's memory, we'll put you down and return their power!"

Morgana laughed again. "You? Just you yourself? Or are you going to somehow get your bandmates to their feet and foolishly fight me again? You can't even stand! Ha, ha, ha! Here, let me hasten your death and you can say hi to Candii for me."

Candii yelled as she watched the screen. "We've got to help them! What do these buttons do?" Candii began frantically pressing things.

"Ooo, please stop changing the camera views. It's making me nauseous." Bell slapped Candii's hands repeatedly. "Yeah, we don't really get involved in mortal affairs. That's kind of a company policy." Bell tried to pull Candii's hands away, but she kept pressing buttons. "Please stop."

The screen kept changing the scene until finally it showed the thirty unicorn pearls floating in the air high above in the rafters of Morgana's lair. Candii froze and stared at them. She had never seen the raw power of the unicorns embodied like the pearls before. This entire adventure helped her realize the unlimited potential her unicorns had. It made her consider that keeping them to herself on her ranch just for her fulfillment may not have been the best use of their talents. Candii thought about how she would never get a chance to find out what her unicorns were truly capable of. That made her very sad. She started to cry again.

"Oh, please don't do that. There's no company policy against crying, but it just makes me uncomfortable," Bell said.

Candii continued to cry and then started to bawl at the thought of her friends dying as well. They did not deserve to die because she dragged them on this doomed trip. She remembered all the nice people she had met along the way and how they would probably be punished for helping her defy Morgana. There was Captain Bing, Krawl, the Spoonman, Mary Sue, Roboxy, Weeoo and Lyla, Pablo, Bob Boberton, Queen Vanillish Moneigh, and even that stupid announcer from the Metal Chef show.

Bell was becoming very uncomfortable, so he patted Candii on the back awkwardly and then left the room, closing the door behind him. Candii continued to cry and felt worse and worse for everything she failed to do when she was alive and the people she failed by not defeating Morgana. Deep inside her heart, she felt a knot building up filled with great sadness. She had never felt this intense, focused feeling before and she was not sure it should still be classified as just sadness.

In that moment, she wondered if this was how Morgana felt all the time. The ogre's words, her disdain and lack of empathy for others, and her lust to have the power to change everything. Was this how Morgana was, and if so, how could Candii herself live like this every day? Candii fell deeper and deeper into despair until she felt her emotions almost melt away in a numbing of her senses.

Something strange happened. The lights in the room blinked out and only the glow of the screen with the unicorn pearls illuminated the room. Candii stopped crying and stared at the screen. She felt a warm presence surround her from all directions. She looked around, but there was nothing there. She rose from her chair and yelped when she realized ghostly images of her unicorn pearls were materializing around her. To her left, to her right, below and above her, transparent copies of her thirty unicorn pearls orbited around her.

She looked closely at one and saw her unicorn's face inside. It neighed at her and she jumped.

"Sparkles? Can you see me?"

Sparkles neighed again in recognition.

Candii shook her head. "But this is impossible! I'm dead and your unicorn pearls are still in Morgana's lair."

Sparkles neighed again and all the other unicorn pearls channeled images of their own unicorn inside them. All the unicorns began neighing and encouraging Candii. Communicating their intentions through their hearts, they told her she should not be sad, that she did so much for them and nurtured them to be so strong. They said they were sorry that they could not protect her or themselves and that they would miss her. They told her to forgive herself.

Candii heard their feelings in her heart. Through their empathetic connection, she truly understood what it meant to forgive herself. In that moment, her heart grew ten times bigger. Possibly literally, but it was impossible to tell. Candii started experiencing feelings that she had never felt before. She embraced a level of empathy that she did not think was possible. She suddenly felt a spiritual connection with many living things around her and even felt their own feelings through her heart.

To her surprise, the unicorn pearls began to glow brighter and more opaque. She checked the screen and saw the unicorn pearls were beginning to fade in the living world. She did not know what was happening exactly, but she reasoned she was summoning the unicorn pearls from across the barrier between the living and the dead.

Outside the room, Bell checked the clock in the hallway and decided Candii probably had enough time to cry out her feelings. He opened the door slowly at first but then swung it wide open when he realized Candii was not there. Instead, there was a huge burning hole in the ceiling.

"Oh, sizzle my sausages!" Bell rushed out of the room and down the hall. He broke the glass on an emergency box and activated the button inside. Sirens wailing and strobes flashing, he ripped off a microphone attached to the side.

"Everybody! We've got a runner!"

Begin Don't Stop Me Now by Queen

INTRODUCTION

Tonight ... time!

Candii was surrounded in an egg-shaped force field of unicorn pearls. Their incredible power emitted a heat that melted the densest of substances. She used their magic to soar upward, higher and higher, not knowing what else to do. To her surprise, she busted through the floor of the eighth circle of the afterlife.

"I guess I'm going the right way!" she exclaimed happily. Around her, she was greeted by a full platoon of magical creatures in riot gear.

"Attention Ms. Candii! Stand down! You are dead and there is nothing you can do about it!"

"Don't stop me!" she cried.

VERSE 1 & PRE-CHORUS

I'm ... you!

Candii felt intense emotion and the unicorn pearls shot away from her. They swirled around the room and knocked all the guards off their feet.

"Code Red! Code Red!" a guard on his radio shouted. "She smuggled magic into the afterlife!"

Hundreds more guards flooded onto the scene around her. Her unicorn pearls spun wildly around and knocked back scores of attackers. Some nimbly avoided them and charged at her.

Candii flinched and the unicorn pearls returned to her. They formed a cocoon of heat and radiated out, blowing everyone away with incredible force. She then wished to rise, and she did. She began to soar upwards again, bursting through ceiling upon ceiling. Finally, she crashed through the floor of the seventh level of the afterlife.

CHORUS

Don't ... all!

She could finally tell the difference between the floors. This one was considerably dingier and the people looked much sadder. "Gross. I'd hate to be sent here!"

Armored vehicles and helicopters approached from the horizon. Candii just wished they would go away, and the unicorn pearls went into action. They swirled out in pairs, colliding softly with the vehicles. They gently lifted them up, up, up. She was not sure where they went, but the unicorn pearls returned to her and pushed her again ever upward.

She soared up through countless more ceilings of brick, granite, and diamond until she burst through the floor of the sixth level of the afterlife.

VERSE 2 & PRE-CHORUS

I'm ... you!

"Ready…aim…fire!"

An army of magical creatures screamed. Rockets and bombs fired around and above Candii. She braced herself for impact but it never happened. She opened her eyes and saw the swarm of ordinance frozen in mid-air. She gave the army a polite wave and pushed upward.

Candii burst through the floor of the fifth level of the afterlife. She was really in the slums now. There were considerably fewer numbers of professional creatures and instead just a bunch of regular people.

"Hey, look at that! She's busting out!" a grizzly familiar looking man shouted.

"Oh shoot!" Candii yelled. "That's John Wayne Gacy!" A mob of people jumped onto her unicorn egg and tried to grab hold.

BRIDGE

Don't ... me!

Candii spun the egg around and flung a great number of people off, but many more were still holding on.

She decided to shake them off with extreme maneuvers, so she soared at breakneck speed upward and onward.

She burst through the fourth, third, and second levels of the afterlife.

INSTRUMENTAL

♫ ♫ ♫

She checked her egg. No more hitchhikers. She sighed with relief but then noticed she was surrounded by a countless number of army personnel led at the front by Bell.

"Yeah, sorry about lying to you," Bell said. "I'm not really some pencil pusher, but the top dog in charge. Don't make me take you down like an animal, Candii! You're so cool! Just turn yourself in!"

"You saw what I saw," she replied. "Nothing in the world or the next will stop me from protecting my family!"

PRE-CHORUS

Ooh ... you!

"Charge!" Bell screamed.

The entire forces of the afterlife rushed Candii's egg and flooded over her. All light was blotted out. She could see only hands trying to pull apart her unicorn pearls. She saw Bell's face, angry with fury. Bell tried to stick their fingers in between two unicorn pearls but was totally unable to.

"We have a system down here, dammit!" Bell roared.

CHORUS x2

Don't ... all!

"Be gone!" Candii cried and a wave of unicorn magic blasted hundreds of personnel and their vehicles far away from her. She soared ever upward toward the final ceiling. It was reinforced with something similar to the unicorn pearls, as far as she could surmise.

Her egg collided and sparked wildly. Candii closed her eyes and wished with all her heart to reunite with the band. The ceiling violently gave way and she broke through.

Candii felt the cool temperature of the living world finding herself under the ocean. She gazed upon her hands. She was a ghastly translucent ghost.

"Wow. I really need to tan more."

Her egg bubbled to the surface and gently emerged from the evening waves. She was just outside the coast of the Land of Rock. She saw Morgana's volcano nearby, so she soared at light speed, streaking through the nighttime clouds like lightning and neared Morgana's lair. She braced herself as she exploded into the throne room.

Her body, lying lifeless and still on the castle floor, evaporated into glitter. Inside the egg, she became corporeal again and free of any wounds.

End Don't Stop Me Now by Queen

Candii cried from within her egg, "Morgana Malevolent! Your reckoning is here!"

"What in the heckin' hamburger?" Morgana shouted as she turned to face Candii. "You're supposed to be dead!"

"Try again, dirt bag!"

"Gladly!" Morgana flicked her wrists but the unicorn pearls did not respond to her. "How did you take them from me?"

"They were never yours to keep. You have no power over them anymore." Candii descended to the ground and dispersed the pearls into a wide circling orbit around her.

"That's fine! Take this!" Morgana shot a searing beam of light at Candii, but one of the unicorn pearls deflected it into a crowd of Morgana's own minions. They wailed and burnt up to a crisp.

Morgana's eyes grew wide. "Candii!" She sniveled as she took steps away from her, wringing her hands together. "We can work this out! I…I never told you why I wanted the unicorn pearls, did I? Why don't we start there?"

"No thanks. No more games." Candii directed the pearls forward. They gently swept up Sir Taco, Thad, and Key in their embrace. Candii then lifted herself up as well and slowly hovered out of the ceiling's gaping hole.

Candii turned back to launch one last magical blast at Morgana. Yet, the witch was not standing defiantly. Instead, she laid crumpled upon the floor, crying over a glowing blue crystalline structure. Candii used her magical empathy power and peered into Morgana's heart. She felt Morgana overflowing with pain and sorrow. Her wails touched Candii's heart in a way she never thought would be possible for such an evil person.

Candii could no longer bring herself to harm the witch any further. "We're going home," she announced. "I'm leaving you here to tend to your wounds. I'm sorry it had to end this way." She looked away. "I didn't think you had any dimensions to you other than evil. I hope you still find a way to achieve your dreams. At least the ones that don't involve killing everyone." She floated out into the night sky.

Morgana threw her hands onto her head and began to pull her hair. "Alone again? After how close I got? I have searched for so long and have found no other way! No, I can't let you take the unicorn pearls!"

Morgana struggled to her feet and threw back her cloak. She thrusted her arms forward and mustered all her emotions of loss and rage into her chest.

To Candii's surprise, it was like a horror movie. Morgana's skin crackled like the Earth's crust exploding with magma. Red and orange beams of light shot out of her and her limbs grew outward. She doubled, tripled, and quadrupled in size into a hulking monster of fiery ash and brimstone. Horns sprouted from her hair, obsidian claws stretched toward the moon, and her long cloak ignited into searing flames wavering in the night's gentle wind.

"Candii!" she howled. "I've never had a true chance at happiness and you horde the power all to yourself. If I must lose myself to wring it from you, then so be it!"

Her mouth swung open. A massive fire ball gurgled and grew inside. She yelped, her insides blistering and scarred, as she spat her desperation out of the castle and after the band.

The fireball grew and grew, filling up Candii's entire range of vision as it staggered forward. It burned as bright as the sun and melted the roof and walls of Morgana's lair. Morgana herself shielded her face from the blazing heat. Candii raised her hand to the night sky and drew down the stars of Orion to create a godly celestial guitar. She strummed it once and deflected Morgana's fire ball back into the castle.

The castle exploded and crumbled into a bazillion pieces. As far as the continent denizens could see, Mount Rock was erupting furiously.

23 Love Endures

Begin Thinking Out Loud by Ed Sheeran

VERSE 1

When ... twenty-three.

Under the rubble, Morgana still lived. What life she had left was fading fast as the magic leaked from her body and her form returned to normal. She crawled through the brick and mortar to find that one treasure she needed most to see.

She pushed stone off the glowing blue crystal that contained the body of her love, Jayce Corgimiester. She closed her eyes and whispered an ancient spell. The crystal began to fade slowly as his body began to warm.

Jayce opened his eyes for the first time in thirty years. He coughed once. Morgana closed her eyes and put her hand on his cheek.

"Morgana," he whispered. "What happened in the courtyard? Are you okay?" He coughed again. "I feel strange."

PRE-CHORUS

People ... am.

"Honey, be still. You're not well." She felt his face beginning to warm again quickly. She knew she had no power to save him at this point, and possibly ever.

Were all her years of toil and regret for nothing? Was she truly destined to fail and die without ever experiencing her dream of a life with her true love?

CHORUS

So ... are.

"What's the matter? Did the headmistress get on your case again?" Jayce asked.

"No, she said she understood."

"Wow, that's uncharacteristically nice of her. So then why do you look like you just got out of a fight?"

Morgana laughed, coughing up on her robes. "Oh, you know, the usual. Just drama and work."

Jayce closed his eyes and nodded. "Of course."

They lay in silence for several minutes. Jayce broke it by asking, "How many decades have I been under?"

VERSE 2

When ... memory.

Morgana's mouth fell open. "You know?"

"You're not the only genius around here," he laughed. "I'm putting it all together now."

"Ah." Morgana sighed. "Then you know about your condition."

"My condition? What about you? You're leaking out of your face."

Morgana wiped the red off her brow. "Never mind that. You have no idea how long I've waited and wished just to hear your voice again. To feel your skin against my hand."

Jayce nodded. "As have I."

PRE-CHORUS

People ... understand.

Morgana tried to lift herself, but she collapsed.

"Don't push yourself," Jayce pleaded.

"It doesn't matter," Morgana said sadly.

"It does. You're reducing the minutes we have left with each other."

Morgana considered it. "You're right. I don't want to lose another second." She laid back down next to Jayce and cuddled up against him. Utilizing great will, Jayce moved his arm over her. His sore muscles barely responded, but he finally pulled her in closer.

CHORUS

But ... are.

Jayce's body heat was getting dangerously hot. Morgana's wrath from thirty years prior was returning to end what it started.

As her consciousness began to fade, she thought about what her mother said before she passed.

"You must fight for every moment to live."

She felt a welling in her heart and she snapped back awake. "I want every second left with you that you'll give me," she said. "Take me into your loving arms."

Jayce did so gently.

INSTRUMENTAL

♫ ♫ ♫

Jayce began to smolder and crackle. He felt no pain because his body had long stopped responding to such a trivial function for a crystalline man. Morgana began to simmer as well, cuddling with a body the temperature of the sun's surface. She took no precaution to cast an insulation spell. Instead, she pushed deeper into his chest.

CHORUS

So ... are.

"Goodbye, my love," Jayce whispered into her ear.

"Goodbye, my one and only," she replied.

Morgana took Jayce's hand and squeezed it tight. They both shone with an immaculate red glow. Their hands melded into one.

The horde of Morgana's remaining minions fled the room as intense heat radiated out and burned everything in its wake. Finally, their two bodies evaporated into scorching steam and dispersed into the air. Their essences intertwined and rode the wind into the night sky.

End Thinking Out Loud by Ed Sheeran

24 Prayin'

Under cover of the night sky, Candii touched down in Jammertown outside of Krawl's vehicle rental shop. She gently placed each member of the band on the ground and then released the unicorn pearls, sending them into her backpack.

Key was first to wake. "Candii. What happened? I thought…"

"Well, you weren't wrong. Let's just say my commitment to protect my family, no matter equine or people, is very strong."

"Fair enough," Key said.

Sir Taco and Thad then roused and jumped to their feet.

"Morgana! Stand back everyone!" Sir Taco shouted.

Thad grabbed Sir Taco. "It's all right! It's over! She's gone. Candii did it."

"She did? She did what?" Sir Taco asked.

Thad scratched his head. "I'm not entirely sure, to be honest. What did happen up there, Candii?"

Begin Praying by Kesha

INTRODUCTION & VERSE 1

♫♫♫ *… become.*

Candii sighed. "I was able to connect with the unicorn pearls from beyond the grave and come back to life." She saw the unicorn pearls react to their mention as her backpack glowed slightly. "I used my new ultimate connection to take control of all the unicorn pearls and defeat Morgana."

"Good riddance," Sir Taco scoffed. "I hope she burns in fiery pits and gets poked by pitch forks for all of eternity."

PRE-CHORUS

'Cause ... farewell.

"No," Candii said in defiance, surprising the band. "Right before I defeated her, I saw something emerge. She was a real person with real feelings other than jealousy and disdain."

Key shook her head. "But she..."

Candii threw up a hand. "Despite the atrocities she caused, I have to believe that she wasn't born that way."

CHORUS

I ... prayin'.

Candii took a seat on the cold, hard ground.

The band joined her.

"On our way back here, I found myself thinking. Would I turn into that if I didn't have all of you? I have an incredibly powerful gift now and I must make sure I use it responsibly. Can I avoid absolutely corrupting like Morgana?"

VERSE 2

I'm ... come!

The band was silent for a moment.

Sir Taco took Candii's hand. "There's no way that'll ever happen to you. I'll always be there for you if you ever need me."

Thad and Key joined their hands as well.

"That's right," Thad agreed. "Key and I will always be there for you."

Candii closed her eyes and nodded.

Her heart welled up.

She was going to be okay.

VERSE 3

'Cause ... name!

Thad saw a shooting star rise from the horizon and dart across the sky.

"Do you think she died in there?" he asked.

Candii considered it. "She had great power, but I'm not sure even she could survive her own strongest magic. Wherever she is, I'm praying that she can come to peace with her demons."

Candii considered her words. On the Continent of the Jam Gods, it was very possible Morgana was literally with demons.

PRE-CHORUS

You ... farewell.

"Please, everyone. Wherever she is, let's wish her well," Candii asked. She squeezed their hands and they tried to think positive thoughts for Morgana.

CHORUS

I ... prayin'.

The band fell silent again. Candii wished with all her heart that Morgana finally got what she wanted. What she needed to be whole.

The unicorn pearls glowed and jiggled in her bag.

Somewhere up in the sky, Candii saw that same shooting star fly across the sky again with another light right behind.

She thought she felt Morgana's presence along with another.

BRIDGE

Sometimes ... forgive!

Candii moved her lips and sang.

CHORUS

I ... prayin'

The band remained silent and held each other's hands for a moment longer.

Finally, Candii picked herself up and dusted the dirt off her clothes. "Well, this is it. We're at the end of our last set list."

"Not so fast," Thad said. "We've still got to return our van keys." He jingled the last remaining piece of their rental from Krawl.

End Praying by Kesha

25 *Raise a Glass to the Good Times*

Begin I Gotta Feeling by Black Eyed Peas

INSTRUMENTAL & CHORUS x4

♫ ♫ ♫ ... *night.*

The band visited Krawl at his 24-hour vehicle rental shop and apologized for totaling his van. Krawl said it was not a big deal. After all, they signed an agreement that required them to pay for the damages. The band had no problem with that; it was only fair.

In Jammertown that night, Krawl called all the band's friends to wish them farewell. Everyone was there: Captain Bing, Krawl, the Spoonman, Mary Sue, Roboxy, Pablo, Bob Boberton, Queen Vanillish Moneigh, and Weeoo and Lyla.

Krawl hosted the party at the classy beach-side resort, Hotel California. The hotel bar's neon lights and dance floor were alive with activity. One by one, all their friends waited to catch up with the band and tell them how their lives had changed since their intervention.

Captain Bing was excited to hear all about their adventure since the last time she saw them.

The Spoonman laughed about his small part in it all. He was just happy that he helped save Candy Town.

Mary Sue told the band that she and the boy were now going steady and it was all thanks to them. Now she was a strong, confident woman.

Roboxy updated the band that her robot army was back on the streets keeping the local mutant sewer rats at bay, which was their original prime directive.

Pablo shared that he had moved on from anger art and was now a sculptor. He had reclaimed some credibility amongst his peers. He still was not back together with Johnny, and that was probably okay.

VERSE 1 & 2 & 3

Tonight's ... again!

Bob Boberton was pleased to report that he had changed his name to Robert and that he was now a totally different person. He worked as the talent manager at The Romp Room. He now managed spreadsheets that contained more than one piece of information. It was very exciting.

Queen Vanillish Moneigh would not stop thanking the band for the performance of a lifetime. She said she had not closed her doors once due to the amount of traffic trying to party there. She was still in the market for NTKG gear and so the band graciously signed a slew of memorabilia she brought with her.

Little Weeoo and Lyla shared that they were happier than they had ever been. They also said that they had never been particularly musically inclined, but they were starting a rock band in their frozen village.

The thought of an all-elf band sent cute-shivers down Key's spine.

PRE-CHORUS

Let's ... it.

The stupid announcer from the Metal Chef show arrived and brought Orangello T. Money and Fire Chief Shannon too. Orangello went on and on about their chocolate covered figs.

Thad ordered a round of figs and dipping chocolate for the whole party and everyone helped themselves.

CHORUS x2

Cause ... night.

Krawl knew they could not have a party without music so he ran across the street and picked up a brand-new set of the loudest and greatest instruments the Land of Rock could offer.

Candii did not need a new guitar since she still had her celestial bass. She donated Krawl's gift to Robert Boberton and told him to give rock a try.

Key was just thankful she had a drum set that was not in a thousand pieces. She had lost her diamond drum sticks, but the store had a great pair, too.

Thad and Sir Taco gladly accepted their gifts.

VERSE 4 & 5 & 6

Tonight's ... again!

The band announced an epic set list and that they would be playing all the way into the morning. Everyone left voicemails at their jobs saying they were going to be sick. Robert laughed because his call just rang Vanillish's phone.

Weeoo and Lyla opened for the band with a little recital. Candii told them they were pretty good! While wind instruments were not traditional rock instruments, who was she to tell denizens of the Land of Rock otherwise?

Robert then took the stage and tried, but failed, to produce anything resembling music during his first experience with a guitar. The band clapped profusely none the less and told him that practice makes perfect. The crowd was also very encouraging.

PRE-CHORUS

Let's ... it.

Roboxy shouted that her robot army had arrived, but this time to party. A bus full of cardboard robots poured into the bar and swarmed the dance floor. They wowed the crowd with their sick robotic dance moves.

With the room reaching a fevered pitch, the band took the stage and began their set list.

Verse 7 & 8

Here ... day!

They played Sex is on Fire, Alive, Lump, The Middle, Eye of the Tiger, We Got the Beat, Living on a Prayer, Go Your Own Way, Devil Went Down to Georgia, Carry on My Wayward Son, More

Than a Feeling, You Oughta Know, Drain You, and Pinball Wizard. And when they were done, they played it again!

CHORUS x2

And ... night.

Early the next morning, the band embarked with Captain Bing back to New Orleans and said goodbye to the Continent of the Jam Gods. Captain Bing was very hungover, but her loyal crew handled the ship with expertise.

Candii laughed as the shore disappeared over the horizon. "We made it, gang!"

Key asked, "What's next for The Non-Traditional Key Gullz?"

"I think that's up to her." Thad turned to Candii. "What are you going to do with your unicorn magic once you return it to your team?"

Candii thought for a moment. She watched the waves under the clear sky rise and fall. "Well, after everything I've done, enjoying retirement on the ranch away from the world is no longer an option. I have been burdened with the truth of what a great power my unicorns have within them. I don't agree with Morgana on almost anything, but she made me realize that in order to deserve my equestrian team, I must practice great responsibility."

The four of them stood silently. They pondered Candii's earned knowledge and what that meant for her.

She turned toward Thad. "Hey, what did you two say you were doing before you came down here?"

"Fighting for social justice and equality," he answered. "You know, normal stuff."

"Let's do some normal stuff," Candii said.

End I Gotta Feeling by Black Eyed Peas

Track List and Credits

1. City of New Orleans
    a. Performed by Arlo Guthrie
    b. Written by Steve Goodman

2. Hungry Like the Wolf
    a. Performed by Duran Duran
    b. Written by Andy Taylor / John Taylor / Nick Rhodes / Roger Taylor / Simon Le Bon

3. Get Lucky
    a. Performed by Daft Punk ft Pharrell & Nile Rodgers
    b. Written by Guy-Manuel De Homem-Christo / Nile Rodgers / Pharrell Williams / Thomas Bangalter

4. Rolling In the Deep
    a. Performed by Adele
    b. Written by Adele Laurie Blue Adkins / Paul Richard Epworth

5 Popcorn
    a. Performed by Hot Butter

6. Spoonman
    a. Performed by Soundgarden
    b. Written by Christopher J. Cornell

7. We Hold Each Other
    a. Performed by A Great Big World ft. Futuristic

    b. Written by Ian Axel / Chad Vaccarino / Daniel Romer / Zachary Lewis Beck

8. Ocean Avenue

    a. Performed by Yellowcard

    b. Written by Benjamin Eric Harper / William Ryan Key / Peter Michael Mosely / Longineu Warren Iii Parsons / Sean Michael Wellman-Mackin

9. I Could Not Ask For More

    a. Performed by Edwin McCain

    b. Written by Diane Eve Warren

10. Wonderwall

    a. Performed by Oasis

    b. Written by Noel Gallagher

11. Fantasy

    a. Performed by Mariah Carey

    b. Written by Dave Hall / Mariah Carey / Chris Frantz / Tina Weymouth / Adrian Belew / Steven J.C. Stanley

12. Downtown

    a. Performed by Macklemore

    b. Written by Evan Flory-Barnes / Darian Asplund / Ryan Lewis / Tim Haggerty / Eric Nally / Ben Haggerty / Jacob Dutton / Joshua Karp / Joshua Rawlings

13. Boulevard of Broken Dreams

    a. Performed by Green Day

    b. Written by Billie Joe Armstrong / Mike Dirnt / Tré Cool

14. Bittersweet Symphony

    a. Performed by The Verve

    b. Written by Keith Richards / Mick Jagger / Richard Ashcroft

15. Animal

    a. Performed by Neon Trees

     b.   Written by Branden Campbell / Christopher Allen / Elaine Doty / Glenn Tyler / Timothy Pagnotta

16. Born This Way

     a.   Performed by Lady Gaga

     b.   Written by Stefani Germanotta / Jeppe Laursen / Fernando Garibay / Paul Blair

17. Any Way You Want It

     a.   Performed by Journey

     b.   Written by Steve Perry / Neal Schon

18. The A-Team

     a.   Performed by Ed Sheeran

     b.   Written by Ed Sheeran

19. Famous Last Words

     a.   Performed by My Chemical Romance

     b.   Written by Frank Iero / Ray Toro / Bob Bryar / Michael Way / Gerard Way

20. Holding Out for a Hero

     a.   Performed by Bonnie Tyler

     b.   Written by Dean Pitchford / Jim Steinman

21. Don't Stop Me Now

     a.   Performed by Queen

     b.   Written by Freddie Mercury

22. Thinking Out Loud

     a.   Performed by Ed Sheeran

     b.   Written by Amy Wadge / Ed Sheeran

23. Praying

     a.   Performed by Kesha

     b.   Written by Kesha Rose Sebert / Ben Abraham / Ryan Lewis / Andrew Joslyn

24. I Gotta Feeling

a.   Performed by Black Eyed Peas

Written by Frederic Riesterer / David Guetta / Stacy Ferguson / Allan Pineda / Jaime Gomez / Will Adams

Play the Prologue

Before the final battle, before the road trip, before the unicorn ranch, there was the world-famous Non-Traditional Key Gullz! Play the computer entertainment game about the band's final world tour over ten years prior to Candii's Quest. And you don't even need a Pretendo 64!

Become a legend...again! The Non-Traditional Key Gullz Return is the sequel to a game that never existed where you, the world-famous drummer Key, must reunite your superstar bandmates and prepare for one final world tour. Featuring over 30 hit classic rock and pop songs from the 1970's to today!

An RPG adventure for all ages!
Download for free at
https://www.choustore.com/chouu/GDSN/GDSN202.html

Band Profiles

Candii

Personality

Full of emotion for everything like gum wrapper commercials, commercials about mattresses, stuffed animals left on the side of the road, the rising sun, the setting sun, the sun sitting in the sky just minding its own business. Everything.

Fashion Style

Loves wearing as little as possible. 'Not-pants' hot pants, a crop top, and some rockin' makeup imbued with just the right amount of glitter: a metric ton. She is a strong, independent woman and don't forget it.

Likes

Unicorns, glitter, and Ed Sheeran.

Hates

Thieves, liars, haters, evil wizards, and spiders.

Blood Type

XOXO

Key Gullz

Personality

Always cracking jokes. Behind her jokey façade lies a person fiercely loyal to her friends. A huge network TV binger and lover of true crime shows. Loves to play the drums and knows she's the best in the world.

Fashion Style

Classic jeans and a tee shirt adorned with roses for this lady. She changes her hair color and style depending on the day of the week or her current mood.

Likes

Sex is on Fire by Kings of Leon, babies, and really campy movies.

Hates

Poop, potty humor, and the fact you're thinking about poop right now because of this sentence.

Blood Type

MURDER

Thad Penguino

Personality

The analytical one. A data miner who sources only the most reliable websites: the convenient first one in the search results. Is very popular among drag queens, they say there's just something about him that begs to be teased.

Fashion Style

Classic-rock ripped jeans and a tee shirt from his old college days. Only dresses up if he has to.

Likes

Swimming, Tias knock-off cheddar tortilla chips, and the Chicago Cubs.

Hates

Ketchup on his Chicago hotdog, people who lie to his face, and people who don't believe in family.

Blood Type

FLYTHEW

Sir Taco

Personality

Always jovial. Even when no one's around and he's alone in a room, he's smiling. Not because he's a borderline psychopath (on the good side of the border, mind you) but because life's too short to frown.

Fashion Style

Aviator sunglasses, a black shirt with a taco on it, and pearly-white shoes.

Likes

All food ever, exploring the unknown, and being there for his friends.

Hates

Waiting in lines, corporate greed, and olives.

Blood Type

TACO

A Note from the Author

$\mathcal{I}$ wrote this book as a holiday gift for my wife. Leading up to the year I wrote and then gifted this, I was notorious for giving bad gifts or sometimes no gifts at all. Clearly all involved found this unacceptable and so a change needed to be made.

Traditions be damned, I decided to skip the regular timing and expectations of regular holiday gift giving and go a less retail route. I thought to myself, "What is something I could do using my talents as they were to make up for all those disappointing holidays and birthdays?"

I am creative. What form would this gift take? Clothing and textiles, drawn or digital art, a movie, song, or even a personal video game? One night I had a dream about escaping from Hell to the tune of Freddie Mercury's *Don't Stop Me Now* which inspired a chapter in this novel. When I awoke, I had the idea to create a track list that would be accompanied with short vignettes to allow the imagination to run wild with a movie playing in your head as you listened to the song.

However, my wife is not terribly creative (sorry, honey) and I knew she might have trouble extrapolating magical or fanciful worlds from a limited prompting. That's when I decided to write something more substantial. I had already been writing a novel of my own for several years and had honed my amateur writing craft to a barely capable level. I decided to give it a go but had some trouble coming up with the right setting.

My first attempt was a star-crossed lover's alternate universe featuring us involved with other people in lives that we were unhappy with. As fate would have it, we are brought to each other and we find happiness in the current arrangement we have in real life. However, it occurred to me halfway through the initial planning of story arcs that my wife may not be pleased reading a story for her that included me with another woman (in any capacity and no matter the end).

With no idea for what to do next, I almost scrapped the idea altogether until a random seedling of creativity sprouted in my mind. I ran it past a friend on the phone, suggesting the musical idea would go great following another cast of fictional characters that already existed within our friend group and to which my wife had a fond affinity to. I could include high energy rock music along with slow romantic songs of her choosing in a literary world entirely free to be explored but also known for being outrageous due to my previous dabbling with it.

After talking out loud for about ten minutes I knew I had something. Over one hundred hours later I completed the main narrative of Candii's Quest and was fortunate enough to finish it early to run it by our other two good friends who have personas in the novel. I'm pleased to say they enjoyed it.

With that final nod of approval, I sent this off to the printer and got it in time for holiday morning and she loved it more than any gift I had ever given or would probably ever be able to produce again. Of course, I'm writing a forward before the actual printing and delivery of said gift so this is all just speculation that I hope comes true. Check in with me if you're reading this and find out how it really went.

Second Edition Note

Thank you for picking up the second edition of Candii's Quest. If you were fortunate enough to have read or obtained a copy of the first edition, published in 2017, then you are a dear friend to me indeed. Otherwise, the rest of you lucky people get to read this second edition note, with no wait, that updates you regarding the delivery of the first edition and how this one came to be.

As planned, the book was delivered on time and prior to December. In fact, it arrived so early that I was able to orchestrate a dramatic reveal at a planned meet-up with the very people who have personas within this book. We convened in early December in Indianapolis, Indiana, to see the movie *The Disaster Artist*, a mockumentary of a favorite movie of our crew, *The Room*. The five of us are able to come together once a year (if the stars align), so this was a momentous occasion for sure.

Prior to our trip to Indy, I reached out to the other three and pitched the idea for the dramatic reveal and then suggested a live reading where each of us would reprise our roles. With that plan agreed upon, we met up in Indy and saw the movie. Later that evening, the book was revealed.

My wife had a feeling. She knew I was up to something for months when I came home and put my nose into my laptop for hours a day. I was secretive and she did get a glance at a few unattended screens from time to time. She wasn't sure what the scope of it was, but she saw a few familiar names which gave her a ballpark idea of the subject matter. As we read Chapter 6 aloud, it was clear that everyone's voice was captured sufficiently. A good time was had by all.

It wasn't until we returned home and my wife began reading the rest of the book as time allowed, that she notified me of errors and typos as far as the eye could see.

I had spent approximately a month editing the book like an amateur rocket scientist, assured that online tutorials and videos could get me to the moon and back, when in fact I had hobbled together a baking soda powered craft that barely brought me into the stratosphere.

This was the beginning of an editing period where my wife affectionately stated, "This book is like the gift that keeps giving!" You see, she loves to edit. Give her any text and she'll point the errors out to you while reveling in the process. So in a way, she has a thing for amateur rocket science.

Here we are now with the release of the second edition which includes all her edits of her own tribute book. I also reviewed the text and enhanced some chapters, tightened some narratives, and fixed a continuity error or two. Some may say that a gift not done right the first time is not a good gift at all. I counter that by saying, "Know your audience. Or I hope you are lucky enough to stumble upon the right one."

Third Edition Tiny Note

This final edition has expanded upon all the characters, many of the action sequences, Morgana's past, Candii's struggle with fatigue and what she must do to Morgana, and many other improvements. Thank you again for reading!

Author's Chapter Notes

Third Edition Addition

New to this third edition are the following chapter notes. Gain insight into my creative process for every chapter. Find out my muses, original plans, and what I did to jazz it all up in this latest edition.

Setting the Stage

I knew that attempting to write a musical book, something that is not exactly common, and one that asked you to read while you listened (something I am not particularly good at) required some explanation. At the very least, I needed to explain myself! But also, I needed to explain the structure I created for this to work.

The original draft was just me, the author, explaining what was going on, but I found a better way with this second edition version where I theme it in-world. The section prior to this, the fake reviews, was a blast to write. Parody will never cease being fun to me.

Chapter 1

Candii's Quest is a story about magic, friendship, hope, and pain. Pain can turn some into fearful animals that lash out at anything that gets close. But it can also steel people into crusaders bent on protecting others from suffering the same fate. The character Morgana is the former and Candii is the latter. We shall see how the two sides of this same coin shape these two differently and how the key to Candii's success is seeing both sides, whereas Morgana has long passed that.

Chapter 2

I really like this song. But besides that, if you've read the backstory of this book, 'A Note from the Author', then you know that there was an entire other concept for this book. This chapter with this song was written and plotted in very much the same way. It is a recycled chapter but with the new character and setting.

There were no musicians in that other concept so in this version of the chapter Candii gets to let her soul shine for a moment.

Chapter 3

This chapter double-header has two songs which makes it maybe the second longest chapter in the book. I intended to rush head-on into what this book will be like early. We got action, music, adventure, teamwork, and quirky characters. I think it sets the tone well enough.

Captain Bing is one of the many guest cameos in this book. She is an honorary member of the real-life Non-Traditional Key Gullz. She joined after the initial creation of the band but was a permanent fixture at Rock Band video game nights after that. I just knew she needed a shout out somewhere.

Interesting tidbit: in the first edition of the book Captain Bing was male. I don't recall why I gender-bended the character, other than perhaps I originally had a different name for the captain and they were a male at the time. Sometime toward the end of writing, I inserted the cameo and didn't think about checking the pronouns.

Chapter 4

We're singing to animals! But first, we meet Morgana, the story's biggest baddie, and get to hear her monologue about her master plan. There are many details she doesn't reveal, but this sets up the main story arc for many chapters to come.

My wife thinks the rock-thrown-into-boob physical comedy gag is the funniest thing. I thought it was okay. A little crude, but it would fit Candii's scrappy personality. This is also one of the first chapters where, upon the second edition, I censored out all the real-life swear words and replaced them with the in-world tradition of elaborate made up swears. I honestly think it's more fun this way.

Chapter 5

One of the themes of the book is that villains are not black and white. They are real people who do bad things, but the 'badness' is a matter of perspective. Here is one of our first examples where a villain has a very good reason for doing what she does. She's been threatened, has a family to take care of, and no reason to risk any of that with a stranger who appears out of the air and tries to wrest it from her. Roboxy will have none of that and she will defend herself.

However, warriors can have a higher code. Respect for one another can supersede other authority, especially when you're taking orders from someone who is threatening you. Candii seems capable enough. Perhaps she can take down Morgana and save them all from tyranny.

Chapter 6

Ah, Candy Mountain. An easter egg to the now ancient dawn-of-the-internet flash animation Charlie the Unicorn. It came out sometime after high school and was very edgy for the time. All those stolen Charlie kidneys!

Spoonman was a song the real-life band loved to play in Rock Band. We didn't know half the words except, "Spoonman!" and "Come together with your spoons." Oh, and don't forget that we had lost the Rock Band drumsticks and had to use metal spoons for a period of time. Again, this song was dear to our hearts.

Chapter 7

Sometimes the good guys win and sometimes they lose. A little risk and uncertainty can heighten the stakes so I wrote this early mortality incident to slow the roll of our heroes.

My wife constantly points out that she believes, canonically, Sir Taco and Candii are an item. I vehemently deny this. In the Candii's Quest universe they are strictly just friends. But that doesn't stop me from flirting with the idea in the last few verses of the song.

Chapter 8

We've got your classic misunderstood misanthrope-turned-villain story here. She wasn't born bad; she was turned that way, right? It'll turn out to be a little more complicated than that. This chapter was fun because of all the action. I really liked the adventure aspect as well since we get to see a few different locations. Since I wrote this book, I've learned a lot more about romance writing and the 3rd edition reflects this much more than previous ones. This gets the point across bluntly that they love each other, but I could have done so much more with it. This song was one requested by my wife. More about this song list in future chapters.

Chapter 9

This was one of the slowest chapters I wrote. I tried to slip in several inside jokes like pocket items, Key's obsession with cute beings, the existence of Tia's chips, and more. I enjoy writing action so I had to deal. Why write a slow chapter if that isn't my forte? Well this is one of my wife's requested songs. I slyly asked for a list of faves and this was like number 1, so I had to make it work somehow. More about this list in a few chapters. This 3rd edition of the chapter has a lot better flow so I'm glad to have taken another whack at it.

Chapter 10

I was personally in a position like the class president and my wife was the Mary Sue. The term Mary Sue is known in the literary world as a character the author creates to fulfill their fantasies. It's not used in the exact correct way here and instead is a parody of that. Mary Sue is not the author, rather she is the reader stand-in for who I originally intended this book to be for. Sort of meta.

Moving on, funny story about this song, Fantasy. During the writing of this book, I asked my wife for a list of her favorite songs. She mustered together a paltry list of no more than five. This was one of them and it turned out it wasn't even the right song. She had confused Fantasy with another hit of Mariah Carey's, I'll Always Be Your Baby. Too bad, too. I also liked that song when I was a youth!

Chapter 11

Wonderwall was the most ubiquitous college bro song you could possibly learn to play back in the 90's and 2000's. The scene I describe with bros playing guitars with ladies fawning around them literally existed back then. The reality was that this was the only song they knew how to play on the guitar, thus making them a bro instead of a true musician.

Despite its checkered past, my wife still liked this song so I threw it in here. I had a lot of fun writing a fight scene so high up. It's also good to get the band playing in front of an audience every so often. That's their whole deal, right?

Chapter 12

Who doesn't love car chases, right? I'm a fan of Macklemore and this song was fun to write to. Car chases in those fast + furious movies can be high adrenaline which is hard to convey in writing, but not impossible. I hope I sent some wind through reader's hair with this one.

Chapter 13

This chapter is maybe one of my bottom three most 'eh'. The cute elves dinner chapter is also in the bottom five. They are sort of filler stories that were being written to match a song.

Also, fun tidbit about the songs chosen. These were mainly Rock Band 1, 2, and 3/Guitar Hero World Tour songs since this entire book is inspired by the plastic guitar game, Rock Band.

Crazy, right? It's basically a polished fan-fiction. But, as far as I know, there are NO other Rock Band/Guitar Hero fan-fictions in existence. So at least I have that market cornered...is that a good thing?

Chapter 14

This chapter is one of my bottom five. I don't know. It's okay. I like that I tied in the window jump from Roboxy's chapter again. I like that I highlighted the contrast of the band's personality with this corporate lifestyle. But there are a lot more chapters with action and fun! So yeah, this one is okay.

Chapter 15

I think this is the longest chapter in the book. With two songs and the pace being frantic, I didn't want to separate them. Fun fact: the sneaking and heist portion is inspired by a level in the video game Payday 2 that my wife and I used to play a lot (the nightclub holdup).

Chapter 16

Cooking shows like Chopped, Guy's Grocery Games, and Iron Chef are a favorite for my wife. I had to include an adventure in this genre. Also, she's competed in a few cooking competitions so it was fun to include a cooking related chapter with my view of what goes on during those. Never has 'too many chefs in the kitchen' actually worked out as well as it did for the band in this chapter.

Chapter 17

The whole '3 judges variety show' trope was still pretty popular when the book came out. I mix that in with the food competition genre and I think we have a really fun chapter. Orangello T. Money is part of an inside joke with our friend group and also is partially inspired by Randy Jackson from American Idol's early days.

This chapter also features cameos of other people we knew at the time. Specifically, Morty and Rashad are based off of guys named Joe and Mike, respectively. The history of how the character names Morty and Rashad came to be is a much stranger story. There's a podcast somewhere out there that describes that in… some detail.

Chapter 18

This chapter is the beginning of the end game. It's short because it was meant to ramp up the action prior to a tragic backstory and then whiplash you back into action. Not much here other than the reveal of a really mad ogre.

Chapter 19

A return to the end of Morgana's backstory. We show how she became the way she was, her tragic backstory, and connect to where we last saw her as a youth at the Magical School.

I received feedback from the first draft that her backstory was too tragic. Her mother struggling with substance abuse still made it in, although it is more fantasy slanted. The original draft had even uglier problems for Morgana and it was too sad. It did not quite match the tone of the rest of the book so I eased up a little bit.

Chapter 20

This chapter includes a song from one of my favorite bands of all time, My Chemical Romance. The song can be interpreted a lot of different ways, but I focused primarily on the idea that we want a legacy when we're gone. For the ogre, he saw Morgana like sort of a child of his. He wants her to live her best life and lets this emotion get in the way of the majority of other's right to live.

This chapter is also one of the highest-octane ones we've had so far. Things only ramp up from here so strap into your seats for the biggest battle.

Chapter 21

Here we have it. The classic hero arc in story telling where they face the big baddie and fall just short. Wouldn't it be boring if they just womped her? No, Candii still has a few lessons remaining to learn before she's worthy of her unicorn's magic back.

Chapter 22

Candii and the band have gained great power. But have they learned to use it responsibly? That can be argued because of this chapter. If Candii had the power to deflect the fire orb so directly, certainly she could have flung it somewhere else and maybe even confined Morgana in some way. Instead, she chooses the path of revenge.

Candii will reflect on her actions in the next chapter. If this wasn't a short novella, I'd go more into it but alas, we're almost at the end.

Chapter 23

My wife was not crazy about how this conflict ended. She didn't want Morgana to die or maybe it was that it was by Candii's hand. Still, narratively I had to put a stop to Morgana's shenanigans and free the people of her influence. I may have gone a different way if I had the experience writing and crafting stories I have today, but back then I was almost at the end of this project and ready to close it out.

A cop out? Maybe. Effective and emotional? You better believe it.

Chapter 24

Candii is filled with conflict. Did she do the right thing. Yes. Did she do it the right way? Maybe not. Now she has a sin to carry even if it may have saved many lives in the future. She tries to reconcile this by honoring what little good was left in Morgana, but it may not be enough to ease her empathetic conscious.

Fun fact: the idea to keep Morgana and Jayce's energy alive somehow (through the shooting star, and since we know there is an afterlife in the NTKG universe) allows me to write a sequel. I'll get more into what that might look like in another note.

Chapter 25

Epilogue party, yeah! Lots of partying. This chapter is like the end of a video game where you go back and talk to all the characters to see if they respond to your victory. It's also a parade of all the quirky characters we met.

The end also sets up the possibility of another sequel. We see where Candii's head might be at and how things could be different in the future.

As for the possible sequel: imagine this! The magic ether that transports the souls of the dead on the continent of the jam gods to the rock afterlife below the island is broken! Ghosts are appearing at an alarming rate and causing quite a stir. The ghost of Morgana Malevolent, accompanied by her boyfriend, Jayce Corgimiester, pays a spiritual visit to Candii of The Non-Traditional Key Gullz and asks for help passing on.

We'd be looking at a buddy-cop comedy with Candii and her ghost partner Morgana solving the case while also hating each other's guts the entire time.

I'm in the development stages right now for a comic book based on this idea. I'm a long way away from having anything to show yet, but stay tuned!

Continent of the Jam Gods Map

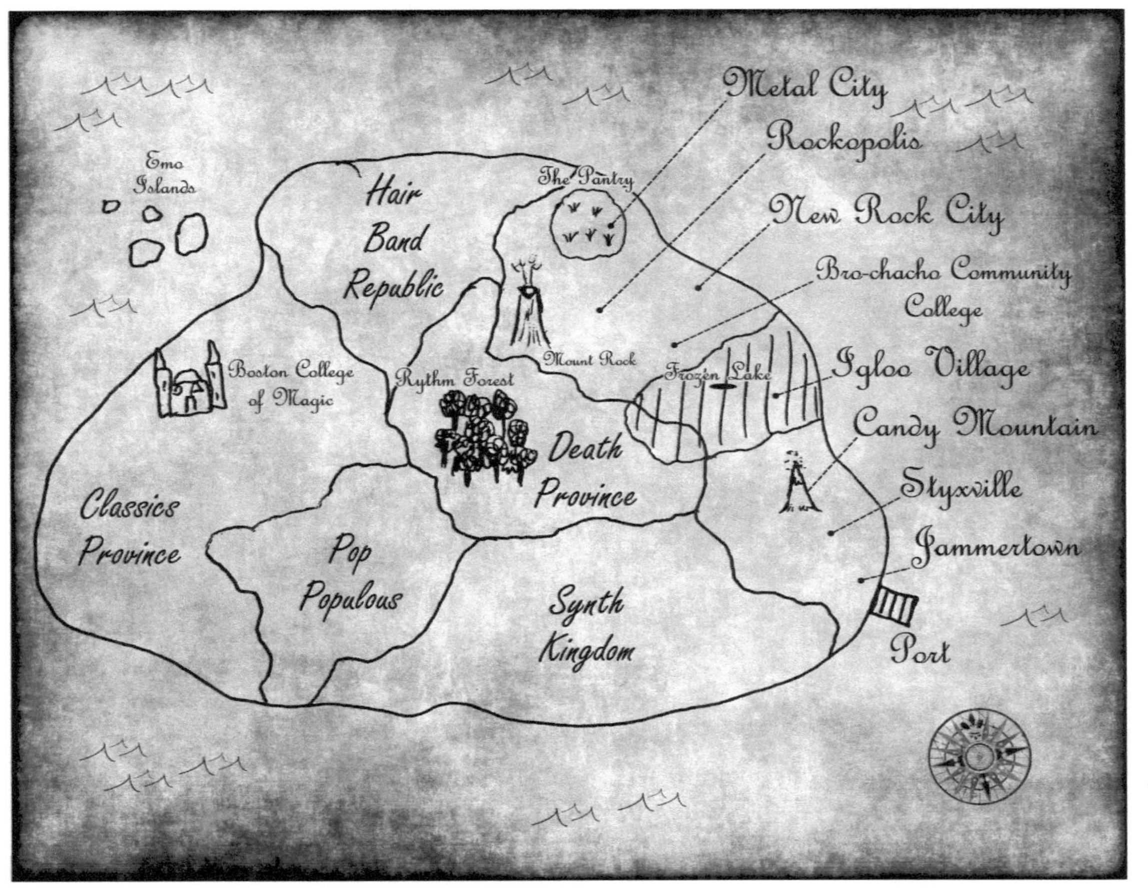

Thank you for reading!

Please visit my website and help me continue to write.

- Leave a review!
- Join the mailing list!
- Go on another literary adventure!

www.choustore.com

Other books by Daniel G. Chou:

Vibrant Steel, a young adult science fiction adventure novel

The Martian Connection, a science fiction romance novella